Forbidden Secrets

MIA SKYE

Editor: Lawrence Editing

Cover Design: Pretty In Ink Creations

Formatter: Cruel Ink Editing + Design

WARNING

This book contains themes with domestic violence, drug addiction, and murder.

PROLOGUE

Tessa

GLASS BREAKING STARTLES me out of my sleep. Eyes wide and body shaking, I lie there, trying to figure out what's going on, wondering what my next move should be. Did someone break in? I turn over to find the other side of the bed empty. Confused, I slowly sit up and search for something to protect myself with.

I come up with nothing.

More shatters come. Who the fuck is this?

I tiptoe closer to the door and slowly open it. The bright light blinds me. It takes a minute for my eyes to adjust. Peeking my head out the door, one of the flowing drapes that hang from the living room window catches my attention. The window is open. Next to it is an ashtray with piles of smoked cigarette butts. Empty beer cans litter the living room. Past the living room, shattered plates, cups, pots, and pans lie all over the kitchen floor.

His back is hunched over the counter with his head in his hands. Confused and frightened at the sight, I tiptoe closer. What is going on?

I reach my hand up slowly and touch his back. "Are you okay?"

A sharp blow connects with my face, and I stumble back. I try to catch my balance, but my head hits the corner of the cabinet.

Shocked at what he just did, no words form. I stand there in silence.

"You ruined my life!" he yells.

Blood is flowing down my long brown hair, dripping onto the floor.

"How could you do this to me? To us?" he bellows.

"How dare you hit me, you son of a bitch? Get the fuck out!"

He slams his fists down on the counter, making me jump. His face is flushed, his nostrils flared out, his jaw tense. His eyes are bloodshot and moving rapidly like he can't control them. I stop and stare in disbelief. I've seen this kind of face before. I've watched someone I love live through this. I've learned to leave the situation alone and walk away until the person is in their right state of mind.

My hair is pulled back and I'm slammed to the ground as I turn around and walk away. "Don't touch me, you piece of shit."

Lifting my head off the ground, I try to control the dizziness that hits me.

"You're a spoiled bitch. This is all your fault."

"Fuck you. I didn't do anything," I yell.

My ribs burn from his kick. Trying to get up, I turn around on all fours and stand up fast. The minute I catch my balance, a hand wraps around my throat. I'm trying to reach his face and push my fingers into his eyes, but I can't. The short length of my arms stops me. I clench my hands in fists and start punching everywhere. One good shot could loosen his hold on me so I can get away. More blows pummel my ribs with his other hand. I'm kicking and throwing my hands everywhere, trying not to give up.

The more I fight, the harder his hand squeezes around my neck. The lack of oxygen is too much for me to keep going. Pictures of my mother flash before my eyes. I never wanted to end up like this.

Opening my eyes to the spinning ceiling fan, I lie there still trying to listen to the sound of him. It's quiet. The burning sensation in my ribs makes it hard to sit up. There is no sight of him. Maybe he passed out? I pull myself off the ground and look around again. Nothing has changed. The open window blows the curtain away, cigarette buts lie next to the window, beer cans all over, glass is everywhere, pots and pans fill the kitchen, and now so is my blood.

I carefully strip the clothes off my body, the stings and burns slowing me down. Naked and alone, I wrap my arms around myself, stepping into the bathroom. I ignore all the mirrors as I head to the shower. I open the shower curtain with the little strength I have left, then step one foot in and the other follows. Letting the water hit my aching body, I wash away the effects of this morning. Lacking the strength to stand, I slowly lower myself down to the bottom of the shower. The water hits me like a waterfall. The tears filling up my eyes are being washed away with the water that flows down my body.

After about an hour of sitting there, I bring myself up to wash my hair and body. With shaking hands, I bring my arms up to reach for the shampoo. The bottle feels heavier than it used to. I scrub myself four times to get all the dried blood off.

Using the bathroom counter to hold myself up, I steady my steps out of the shower. Raising my head as I wipe the steam off the mirror, I'm faced with a complexion I don't recognize. I examine the face I once knew. Every little crevasse has some kind of marking, some kind of color. A red handprint has formed on my neck.

I stare at the brown eyes that once held hope that this would never happen to her, hope that she would never end up like this. Smart enough to know the signs. I catch a glimpse of the person who used to be under there. I tell her this will be the one and only time anyone will ever lay their hands on her.

CHAPTER ONE

Tessa

I LEFT the same night my world turned upside down. I refuse to be his victim. Another victim that falls for repeated apologies. Growing up and watching it with my own eyes was bad enough. I always told myself I will let nothing like this happen to me. Little did I know it's more common than you think. So, I filled my car up, pulled all my savings out, and hit the road.

Saying goodbye to my grandparents was the hardest part. A battered body is what I didn't want them to see. So I couldn't say goodbye to them in person, to avoid worrying them. I told them I had a work opportunity far away and left. I'm hoping they forgive me. My grandma always said she raised me to know right from wrong and what consequences follow if I chose the wrong. I'm now on the phone, explaining a made-up story to her.

"I don't understand how you don't even know where and what exactly you will be doing. Who picks up and leaves without asking questions? And what about what's his face you were living with?" she asks.

"We broke up, and I didn't want to dwell on the breakup, so I thought this would be a good chance to get over him and not be in a limbo relationship," I say.

"You broke up? When did this happen?"

The pit of my stomach hurts with all these lies I keep telling her. I don't want my grandparents to worry. How does someone go about telling the only parents they have that their sweet ol' boyfriend turned out to be someone he's not? She trusted me with my decision, and this one decision gave me consequences I now have to live with. This is the best story I could come up with.

"About a week ago. I planned to tell you once I moved out and found a new place to live. I didn't want you to worry."

"Oh, honey, you know I only worry because I love you. I trust you're making the right decision. You better call me every day, though."

"I will. How about we write letters back and forth to each other like we did when I was younger? I know you miss that."

"Oh, I would love that. You're so sweet to always think of me and what makes me happy. I miss it very much. It will give me something to do since your grandpa rarely talks to me. Oh man, what am I going to do without my weekly visits with you now? I guess I'll have to take up writing you a letter on that day."

I let my grandma ramble on about her day-to-day life. She and my grandpa have been married since she was sixteen and he was twenty. My grandma lived in such a strict household, she hurried and married my grandpa so she could have more freedom. A few years later, a pregnancy surprised her. That took up all her freedom. They both lived a pretty decent life considering the shit show my mother gave them and then having to raise me. It worked out well having my mother at a young age because they were still pretty young and active when they took me in full-time.

They've been retired for a while now, and each of them has their own life. My grandpa is so quiet it bugs my grandma. She always says she feels like she's living alone. But she has learned to fill her days up. Church is on Sunday, followed by a Sunday dinner with me. Laundry day is Monday. Tuesday, she cleans the house. On Wednesday, she works in her garden. Thursday, she goes to the salon to get her nails done and her hair washed and curled for the weekend. Talk about bougie. Friday, she plays bingo with her friends. Saturday, she leaves open for whatever she feels like doing.

My grandpa, on the other hand, sits in his shed all day and night, building random stuff with random materials. He made garden decorations resembling a road runner using small hand-held shovels. He's made wind spinners out of beer cans. It's so random, but they always turn out good. He usually helps my grandma with the garden and the cleaning around the house. But sometimes she hates it because he gets in her way. By the end of the night, they both cozy up together in their den and watch their shows. They're her shows mostly.

The second I turned eighteen and graduated high school, I moved to have my freedom. Even though they let me do whatever I wanted. My mother taught me what not to do while growing up, so I didn't get into trouble. It's every kid's dream to turn eighteen and move out and live on their own, so that's what I did with my best friend. It gave my grandparents a chance to take their motorhome out and travel around the States. Friends and family called them road runners because they never stayed home. Their friends are from all over the world. They have more friends than me.

"Yes, Grandma, I promise to call you once I get there and write to you every week," I say.

"Okay, sweetie, be safe. I love you."

"I love you too."

I left without saying a word to anyone, not even my best friend Mila, who I've been friends with since fourth grade. But I don't know if I would consider us best friends anymore. Our lives have changed and we're out of touch. She got married and started a family. I only got into a serious relationship about a year ago. Saying that to myself makes it sound so pathetic. Can a year-long relationship be serious? Living together was something I only considered in this relationship. A lot of good that did. Look at me now. I'm running away. I haven't had time to sit and process everything. I left that morning, only stopping to rest before hitting the road again.

CHAPTER TWO

Tessa

UP AHEAD, I see massive red rocks. I take the exit and go in that direction. The farther I travel, the more intrigued I am. Large red rocks with many figures appear. Some have an arch form. Some towering and pointed rocks appear as if boulders are piled on top of each other and built together. It's something I've never seen before. I turn onto Main Street and spot a sign that says Moab. I park behind the sign and a hot burn hits me the moment I step outside my car. It's scorching. I feel like the sun is only a foot away from me, and it's melting me. The heat reflects off the sand, making matters worse.

Placing my arm above my eyebrows to try to block out the sun, I look around and hardly see anyone in sight, just a few people coming in and out of establishments on Main Street.

As I get back into my car and head toward Main Street, I observe the small and secluded location. There are many shops, restaurants, and hotels. The sidewalks near the buildings are busy with people coming and going. They might be the locals. I pulled into The Best Western Hotel and decide to stay the night. It's small and doesn't look like it draws a lot of attention.

The sound of children running and laughing down the hallway wakes me up. I lie here, staring at the light streaming through the blinds, listening to the children's mother shushing them and instructing them to return to their room. I have no memory of falling asleep. My stomach churns with a growl. I reach down and clutch my stomach, hoping to quiet the growling. My phone shows it's eight in the morning, which means I slept for twelve hours. My stomach growls once again. I haven't eaten since yesterday morning. I didn't have the energy yesterday. As soon as I got into my room, I showered, lay down, and fell right to sleep. After a few weeks of driving, I knew my body needed it.

Shielding my eyes from the outside light as I step out onto Main Street, I search for a place to eat. My sunglasses are useless since the sun is so bright. Everyone around me is in tank tops, shorts, and flip-flops. So far, all the girls I've seen have their hair up. I'm in a long-sleeved shirt with my long brown hair streaming in front of me. I look dumb. The bruises on my legs were minor and healed, allowing me to wear shorts. I'm still waiting for the rest of my body to heal.

Up ahead, I see a sign that reads Corner Café. Coffee. I need coffee.

I walk in and the aroma of coffee beans fills my lungs. This café is relaxing. It's filled with small, black, round tables and black chairs. Green plants decorate the wooden walls. A small line is forming to the left, ordering from the menu above the register. The cash register's countertop is white-and-black marble. Next to it is a refrigerator stocked with various pastries. After reading the sign that said "Grab a menu and sit," I found myself in a back corner, staring at everyone in front of me.

"What can I get started for you?" The waitress's name tag reads Cheri.

If I'm going to stay here, I better try to make acquaintances. A foot in the door could help me secure a job and a place to live.

"Hi, Cheri, can I get a cup of coffee to start out?"

"Any cream or sugar?"

"No. Just black."

"I see. You like it rough around the edges," she says with a wink.

Laughing, I nod in agreement. Cheri is a middle-aged outspoken woman. She voices her thoughts without hesitation.

Scanning through the menu, everything looks good. Sweet and savory makes my mouth water.

Cheri sets my mug down and pours the coffee. "What can I get for you?"

"Can I get an order of the Nutella stuffed French toast and an order of the hash skillet?"

"You're a little thing. Are you sure you can eat all that?"

Handing her my menu, I say, "Don't underestimate a small girl's appetite."

Cheri walks away laughing.

I glance to my right, where they have baked goods. They look amazing. My sweet tooth might be difficult to control. I blame my grandpa.

People come and go for their morning coffee. Others are sitting and typing on their laptops, attempting to eat something with every spare second. If I had a job that allowed me to work from a laptop, I would spend my day here. It has a soothing atmosphere. It beats going into the office with all the regular office dramas.

After enjoying my coffee and breakfast, Cheri stands next to me and swipes my card.

"Cheri, do you know anywhere that is hiring?"

I hope this place is hiring. Working at this charming café would be amazing.

"Not off the top of my head. Are you looking to stay here?" she asks and hands me back my card.

"If I find a place to live and work, then yes."

"What brought you over here?" She takes a seat on the chair in front of me. The morning rush looks like it's slowing down.

"I was trying to find somewhere new to live."

"All by yourself?"

"Yup. Just me. Would you guys be hiring?"

"No. This place is never hiring. Our small group has been here for years and we're not going anywhere. I'll keep my eye open for you, though."

"I appreciate that."

Standing up as I take the last sip of my coffee, Cheri stops and turns back to me before heading to the back of the café.

"You know what? I think the Antique Shop is hiring. The older lady working there wants to take it easy. She's looking for help. Her name is June."

"Where can I find the antique shop?"

Cheri leads me to the front of the café and points right. "Head down two blocks, cross the street, and you'll see it."

"What's it called?"

"Antique Shop."

"Yeah, what's the antique shop called?" I ask again.

"It's called Antique Shop." She looks at me with a grin.

"Oh." I chuckle.

Cheri laughs and pats me on the shoulder. "I heard it makes it less confusing for tourists."

I shrug my shoulders. "Okay then, thank you."

"What was your name again?" she asks.

"Tessa."

"It was nice to meet you, Tessa. I better get back to work. I'll see you around." She pulls me into a hug. Shocked at first, I loosen up and reciprocate the hug back. People are friendly here.

A squeaky noise comes from the door as I walk into the Antique Shop. I take a couple more steps inside, listening to the floor creak. The shop has an old, musky smell to it. I'm thinking the building was built in the 1900s. The shop has most everything you can think of: clothes, jewelry, furniture, decorations, and books. I'm drawn to a rose quartz heart-shaped crystal. Growing up, my mother collected various stones and crystals.

"Can I help you?"

Turning around, I see a little old, glamorous lady standing upright. She has to be around four-foot-eleven. I'm not tall myself, standing at five-foot-one, but she makes me feel like a giant. She has black slack pants on and a pink top with beaded pearls around her neckline. "Hi. Are you June?"

"Yes."

I reach my hand out to hers. "I'm Tessa." Her hands are so soft and dainty I almost feel like I'm going to break them. But they have a softness to them. Almost like my grandma. It makes me miss her and my grandpa.

"I heard you may be looking for some help. I recently moved here and I'm trying to find a job."

June looks at me with raised eyebrows in questioning. "Why would you move here?"

"Why not?" I ask.

"No one moves here. It's too touristy and hot as hell when summer hits. The only people who live here are the ones born and raised here."

Doesn't look too touristy to me. Who would come here in the summer, anyway? It is too hot to visit. And when winter comes, it's too cold. I'm assuming.

"I'm looking for a fresh start somewhere."

She gives me a side-eye. "A fresh start. You're so young. What kind of fresh start do you need?"

Geez, she's very judgy. "If you don't need anyone, I can look somewhere else. I heard you were looking for extra help," I say with a huge smile. Maybe I have to kill her with kindness.

"No, no. Don't get your panties in a bunch. I'm just asking."

A snort comes out of me as I try to hold in my laugh after that comment. After she hears me snort, she gives me a stern look and puts her hands on her hips.

My eyes go wide and I stop laughing. "Sorry. I've never heard anyone say that before."

She turns her back to me and starts heading toward the back of the shop. Confused, I stand there, watching her leave me behind.

"You coming or what?" she yells.

"Yeah," I call out. I follow her toward the back of the shop and find her sitting behind a counter with a cash register. The cash register is an antique.

"Does that work?" I ask, pointing to the register.

"Of course. How else do you think I ring people up?"

I shrug my shoulders.

"When would you like to start?" she asks.

"Ugh. When do you need me to start?"

"Now. I would like to see how you do during our slow period before the busy season picks up again, in case you're not a good fit for me."

Talk about honesty. "Okay. I can start now."

She places a pen and paper on the counter. "I need you to fill this out."

I reach for the paper and realize it is a W-4 form. "You're hiring me just like that?"

"Were you expecting a sit-down interview?"

"Kind of. I guess."

"Anyone can handle this job. It's easy. Someone walks in,

grabs what they want, you ring them up, and then they're on their way out. It's not that hard. Unless you can't unpack or carry heavy stuff? I have a contact who delivers inventory as needed. He does the heavy lifting. You do the rest. Unboxing and setting it up on the floor. You're a pretty little thing, but so am I, and I have been able to handle this store since my parents got too old to run it. That was thirty-something years ago."

I turn around to the sound of the door squeaking, and the floor creaks.

"Fill it out or don't fill it out. I'll be right back," she says.

I fill everything out but skip the address part. That's next on my to-do list since now I found a job. I don't even know how much I'll get paid.

"So what will it be? Staying or going?" she says as she approaches me and takes a seat on the stool behind the cash register.

"I would like to take the job. I have one problem, though." She doesn't ask what the problem is. She stares at me with a blank expression. I can tell she keeps to herself. She doesn't have many people skills. How does she manage being around people all day? "Since I barely moved here, I don't have an address yet. Can we hold off on it until I find somewhere to live?" She's still staring at me like she's not one bit amused by my life. "Do you know anywhere that's renting?" I ask.

June turns her back to me, hops off the stool she was sitting on, and walks away. This again? Do I follow her?

"Are you coming?" she yells.

"Yeah." I walk behind the counter and make a left turn to a set of stairs. June is nowhere in sight. She's fast for her age. Walking up the stairs, I step into what looks like a studio apartment. June opens the blinds and brings in sunlight. Then she pulls a lever to bring down a bed from what looks like a closet.

"It's not much, but this could help you get started. It has been years since anyone lived here, so it needs work. This is a Murphy bed. You can raise or lower it. That over there is the bathroom." She points behind me.

I walk to the door and open it. It has the standard toilet, sink basin, and a small corner shower. I hear noises coming from the kitchen and see June turning on the gas stove with a match. It lights right up when she puts the lit match toward it.

"I wanted to make sure the stove still worked," she says. She walks a couple feet over and opens a small fridge with a top freezer about the height of her. "It's up to you how much you want to clean and paint. It's yours if you want it."

I'm blown away by her generosity. She appeared uninterested in me or my life a few minutes ago.

"It's perfect. How much is the rent?"

"Let's do four hundred dollars."

"Oh wow, four hundred dollars is great."

She walks away from me. "I'll give you the keys when you come back down."

"Can I get the address for this place?"

June's annoyed face looks at me once again with a blank stare. "For what?"

"Umm, mail."

"Oh no, the only mail that comes through here is what the shop gets. You'll have to go to the post office. Like how we used to do it in the good ol' days."

"Really?" I say, questioning why it would matter.

"Yes. I'm almost eighty years old. I don't need to learn the ways of you kids. You kids should learn how we did it back then. Now every kid I see has some piece of technology in their face. It's pitiful."

I stare at her, confused. What does this have to do with anything? I better just go with it and not push my luck, and she's almost eighty. She looks good for her age. But I bet she's at that point where whatever she says goes.

"Why are you staring at me like that?" she exclaims.

Startled by her tone of voice, all I can say is "ummm."

"Come on, spit it out. I've been around the block longer than you. Nothing will hurt my feelings at this point. I got tough skin." She pats her chest.

"I was admiring how good you look for almost eighty."

"Yeah, well, not having the stress of a husband will do that to you."

"You've never been married?"

"Came close once, then I came to my senses." She turns her back toward me and heads downstairs. "I've been up here long enough. I'll see you downstairs."

She's a little spitfire. I always heard the smaller you are, the more attitude you have. I never believed it until now.

CHAPTER THREE

THIS CRIPPLING PAIN shoots through my stomach. It took me all day to move my stuff from my car to the studio and get everything put away. I haven't stopped once to eat, meaning I haven't eaten since the morning. I need to stop doing that. The sun has set, cooling the day. If it weren't for the swamp cooler in this place, I would be way too hot.

Right after June closed her shop, she came back up and dropped off pillows, sheets, and blankets. She has such a kind heart that she doesn't like to show. She told me to start work on Monday, so I could move everything in. Tomorrow is Sunday, and the shop is closed.

I search for food options on my phone. Everything is within walking distance here. Which I rather like. It's simple to get up and go without having to deal with parking. I scroll around and come to a brewery that looks promising. They stay open till 2:00 a.m. Luckily, I'll have time to shower off all my sweat.

When I walk into Cruz Brewing Co., I hear live music. A band performs on stage to my right. The place is full. Booths line the left wall, with tables and chairs in the center. I'm waiting to be seated in front of the hostess stand. I don't think I'll be able to get a seat here. Every table appears to be occupied. This must be the place to be on weekends.

A blond-haired girl with big boobs bouncing with every step she makes comes up to the stand. "Hi, how many?"

"Just one. Me. It doesn't look like there are any chairs available," I say with a raised voice so she can hear me over the music. The music is so loud. I can tell people are trying to talk over the sound.

"I can probably get you seated at the bar. Give me a minute while I go check."

I nod and watch her walk to the back of the restaurant. There is a bar, but even that looks full. I turn and acknowledge the group walking behind me. Maybe I should find somewhere else to eat, but everything looked closed when I was walking over here. This might be why they're busy this late; they're the only ones open.

The hostess comes back up and says, "I have one of my guys making room for you at the bar. Follow me." We get to the corner of the bar where an iPad is sitting up on a stand. A guy has a debit card in his hand, ringing someone up. "I hope this is okay. I know it's in the corner and by the register, but we didn't want to turn you away, so we cleared some stuff up for you."

"Yes, this is fine. I don't think I'll stay long, anyway."

She hands me the menu. "One of the bartenders will take your order."

I sit down and turn toward the bartenders. They are all serving drinks to the servers who are awaiting their table orders. Everyone at the bar is either eating or watching the band. The band is playing "Hotel California." This is the type of music I grew up listening to. Memories of my mother flood back to me.

She would always sing along to this music and pretend to play the guitar.

"What can I get you?" the bartender asks.

"Can I get whatever your most popular IPA is?"

Nodding, he pours me an IPA in a pint. "Can I get you any food?" he asks as he hands me my beer.

"A bacon cheeseburger and some fries?"

He takes the menu from me. "I'll have that right out."

I smile at him and turn back around toward the band with my beer in hand.

I'm always aware of the bartender who took my order because every time he approaches the register, I'm inclined to look over at him and make eye contact. It only happens with him and not the other bartenders. He has sandy-blond hair tied back in a ponytail and is tall and well-built. His blue eyes stand out against his tanned skin, almost like a sky blue. When we catch each other looking at one another, both of us get this grin on our faces.

After my third beer, I realize I stayed longer than I thought I would. A buzz came on and I was enjoying the atmosphere. It's been a while since I had this much fun. Since that night, it's been nonstop. The brewery is becoming less busy. People are leaving one by one and calling it a night. The blond hostess approaches and takes a seat next to me.

"Hey, Cruz, can I get a beer now?" she asks.

He turns and glances around before pouring her a beer. I'm guessing that employees can drink once it's close to closing time. All the other bartenders and waitresses are following her lead.

I swing my stool around to face the band again. They're looking a little worn out, too.

"I thought you weren't going to stay long."

I move my gaze to her. "I wasn't, but I was enjoying the atmosphere."

"Yeah, this place gets pretty busy on the weekends because of the live bands."

"I can see why. They're pretty good."

"Why are you alone?" she says.

The bartender places a burger in front of her, and she picks it up and takes a big bite.

"I just moved here."

She scrunches her eyebrows and says, "To here? Alone?"

I'm second-guessing my choice to stay. Everyone questions it except for Cheri. She didn't question it. That's two out of three. What's with this town if everyone questions me about moving here?

"Yes. I wanted to start over somewhere new."

"Why alone?"

"I have no one else."

She gives me a questionable look but turns her head back and takes a chug of her beer. The awareness of the bartender hits me again, and we make eye contact.

"Can I close my tab?" I ask.

"Yes, Tessa, right?"

I nod in agreement.

As I'm about to get off the stool, the hostess says, "Some guys from work are going to have a little get-together after we close up here. Do you want to come?"

"Maybe another time. I'm tired from the move," I say as I scoot off the stool.

"Okay, whenever. My name is Ashley, by the way."

"Tessa. It's nice to meet you. Thanks for the invite." I give her a small wave and head out.

"Anytime. I'll see you around."

Nighttime here is pretty dead around this time. It's almost two in the morning, and only a few people are out. It's so quiet—almost an eerie feeling, but also relaxing.

"Have a good night."

I jump back to the opposite end of where the voice came from. My heart is pounding through my chest.

"Sorry, I didn't mean to scare you."

It's the bartender I kept making eye contact with. He's coming out from the alleyway in the dark. The light from the pole above me doesn't shine that bright down there. "It's okay. I didn't see you there. Why are you standing there in the dark?"

"Just making sure no one is passed out in the alleyway."

"Oh, I see. That's nice of you."

"Well, have a good night," he says and heads inside.

"You too."

CHAPTER FOUR

Cruz

I HAVEN'T SEEN her in a couple of days. Even thinking of her makes me smile. There was some sort of nudge pulling me toward her. I wasn't supposed to be working the floor at my brewery that night. I've got guys for that. I was in my office doing inventory when I took a brief break behind the bar. Then Ashley walked over and asked if we could make room at the bar for one more person. Why would she ask that? She knew the bar's capacity and that it was full. But she didn't want to say no to this individual. I asked why. She said that she was here by herself, with a sad expression on her face. So I changed a few things around and carried out a barstool from the back.

She captured my attention the moment I laid eyes on her. There was something about her. Something so familiar. I've seen that kind of sadness before—a sadness I never wanted to see again. I wanted to know more. I had to know more. So I stayed on the floor and worked behind the bar. Everyone was confused and kept questioning why I was working while we were fully staffed. I told them I needed a change of scenery. All the guys frowned at me and questioned my motive. My motive was here. Tessa. I wasn't planning on spending the rest of the night working at the bar. But it was even more difficult to call it a night when those enormous brown eyes stared at me every time I came close. They attracted me like a magnet. So I continued to work.

The only reason I walked outside to see whether anyone was passed out around the building was to make sure no one followed her. Given the number of tourists, this town is safe. But in actuality, I wanted to see her one last time.

CHAPTER FIVE

AFTER MY FIRST day on the job, I head out to the post office to drop off the letter I had written to my grandma. This heat is terrible. Relaxing in a pool sounds nice. Good thing everything is nearby and within walking distance.

June didn't work me too hard. She showed me around and taught me how to use her antique cash register. She said the antique store has been running since her parents opened it up. They used to have a friend who would go to yard sales and consignment stores and pick out unique items. This friend of hers has his own antique store across the country, and anything he wouldn't sell, he shipped over here. When he passed away, his kids took it over and now sell items online. June doesn't believe in online stores, so that was out of the question when they wanted to set her up on it.

June never had children. I'm curious about who will take over her store after she dies. She's in great shape for her age. I'm sure she has a lot more time left. She appears to be deeply attached to the store. No other relatives of hers are here. June has no siblings either.

As I enter the post office, I'm knocked off my feet and my ass hits the ground.

"I'm so sorry. I wasn't watching. Are you all right?"

It's the same guy from the bar. To my surprise, he appears delighted to see me.

He reaches his hand out toward me. I take his hand in mine, and he helps me up. I situate myself. "It's okay. I'm fine."

"You were at the brewery the other night? Tessa, right?" he says as he reaches down, picks up my grandma's letter, and hands it to me.

Embarrassment causes my cheeks to flush. He most likely remembers me making eye contact with him all night. "Yes," I mumble.

"I thought you looked familiar. Are you still visiting?"

"No, I live here now."

He doesn't give me a questionable look like everyone else has. Instead, a slight smile appears on his face. "Come by the brewery tonight and have dinner on the house. Since I ran into you."

"You don't have to do that. I know it was an accident."

"I know, but I want to." He takes a few steps backward. "I have to run. I'll see you later tonight."

"Okay. See you." I give him a small wave.

After contemplating all evening about going to eat at the brewery, I'm here a few hours before midnight when it closes. I didn't want to be a bother for free food because one of the workers ran into me. But then I remembered Ashley, and she seemed like a cool person, and I need to meet new people.

Ashley is sitting at the hostess stand as I walk in. "Hey, you're finally here?" she says with a cheerful tone.

I scrunch my eyebrows, giving her a questionable look.

"Cruz told me you were coming in, and everything is on the house for you tonight," she says.

I nod, confused. What kind of worker can call the shots like that? I don't want to get him in trouble. Realization hits me. Cruz Brewery. He's not just a regular worker, he's the owner. Embarrassed it took me this long to figure it out. I keep my thoughts to myself.

"Follow me." She sits me at a small booth close to the bar. I look over at the bar for Cruz, but he's not there. A few minutes later, Ashley returns to my table.

"Do you know what you want?" She slides into the booth on the other side of me.

"I thought you were the hostess?" I ask.

"I do a little of everything on slower nights."

Not many people are here. Given how late it is, I imagine almost everyone is going to bed right now. It is a weekday. "I'll have a bacon cheeseburger and an IPA."

"Coming right up."

There is no live band today, but music is playing over the speakers. More of a slower country song is on.

Ashley comes back over with two plates and slides into the booth. She reaches over and sets my plate down.

"Do you mind if I eat with you?" she says.

"Sure." It's kind of nice to have her sit with me. I haven't been one to go out alone before. This move is different. I'm all alone, and I'm forced to do things alone. It wasn't awkward at first, but everyone wondering why I moved here made me a little uneasy. I watch her take a huge bite from her burger. For how slim her figure is, she sure can eat a lot. So can I. I don't consider myself slim, if you know what I mean. I have a little fluff that distributes around my whole body nicely. I've never been too concerned about my figure.

"So what's up with you and Cruz?" she asks.

"What do you mean?"

"He never invites a girl to eat here, let alone put it on the house."

"Oh. Well, we ran into each other at the post office, and he accidentally knocked me on my ass. He's just being nice to apologize," I say, taking a bite of my burger.

She shakes her head as if that's not it.

"What?" I say.

"It's still not like him to do that. He's a nice guy and all, but he rarely messes with the locals. Well, you're not technically a local, but you have recently moved here."

"Why doesn't he mess with the locals?"

"It's a small town. Everyone knows everyone's business. He likes to keep his business to himself."

"I see. Can I ask you something?"

She nods.

"Why is it so weird to everyone that I moved here? They don't come right out and say it, but their expressions give it away."

"People who move here alone or have no family here are usually running away from something."

My eyebrows rise, and I'm choking on the beer that went down the wrong tube. There is no way they would know anything about me this soon. My heartbeat races.

"Don't worry. We know nothing about you. All I'm saying is that's usually the case." She gives me a wink.

"Why would moving here show someone is running away from something?" I say with a shaky voice.

"It's a small town. There isn't much room to grow here. All businesses are family owned and have been for years. There aren't any corporate jobs over here. You have to be okay with working at a place around here, or you move away. Usually, people move away after high school to go to college and then find their way from there, but they rarely ever come back."

"Why hasn't this small town grown?" I question.

"Do you not know where you moved?" she says with a questionable grin.

My eyebrows draw together, confused about what she is asking.

"This is a tourist town. It's not too busy right now because it's too hot to go outside for long periods. Soon it will pick up once the temps go down. Do you not notice what surrounds this town?" she says.

"This town gets that busy just to hike these rocks?"

She lets out a small laugh. "You didn't research before you moved here. There is hiking, skydiving, rock climbing, biking, and rafting. There is a lot to do here. People from all over the world come here."

A sudden chill runs down my body. That's great. I thought I moved to a small enough town that no one knew of. Come to find out, this town is popular. Suddenly, I'm not so hungry anymore. I set down my burger and look away from Ashley, observing everyone around me. This whole time, I thought they were all locals.

"Hey, whatever it is, you don't need to be nervous."

I turn back and smile at her.

"Were you born and raised here?" I ask.

Ashley slides out of the booth and grabs both of our cups. "Hold that thought. I'm going to refill our beers."

My eyes follow her to the back of the bar, wondering where Cruz is. I thought he would be here, given he said my meal was on the house. I wonder what his story is. If he was born and raised here. Damn it, now I wonder what everyone's story is.

My gaze lands back on Ashley as she sets our cups down on

the table. "The answer to your question is yes, I was born and raised here. I now live here alone. My family moved away to Colorado. I moved away with them at first, but I didn't like it. So I moved back and have been here ever since." She scoots herself back into the booth. "This town speaks to me. I don't belong anywhere else. I'd like to ask you about your background, but I'm afraid you won't tell me."

I keep my gaze away from her and remain silent. I'm glad she's talking to me, but she is still a stranger to me. I'm not sure I want to say anything.

I look over toward the front door as I hear someone walking through. Broad shoulders appear as he walks in with his head and chest high, as if he owns the place. It's Cruz. He notices Ashley and me sitting together and walks over to us. I turn my head back around and notice Ashley eyeballing both of us.

"Hey, I'm glad you came in. How is Ashley treating you?" he asks.

"Good, she's keeping me company," I say with a slight smile.

"How else would I have treated her, Cruz?" She smirks.

"I'm giving you shit." He laughs. "Remember, this is on the house. If you need anything, let me know. I'll be in the back. I have some work I need to finish up." He gives me a wink and heads toward the back. I watch him walk away, admiring his figure. He's very built and has to be at least six feet tall. No wonder he knocked me down like I was a feather to him. He's about a foot taller than me.

Ashley clears her voice, pulling me out of distraction. "What ya looking at?"

I turn and face her, grabbing a fry to hide my blushing cheeks. Ashley is still staring at me, waiting for me to answer. "What? I can't help it. He's good-looking. Wait, are you two together?"

Ashley laughs. "No. He's like a brother to me. I grew up with him."

"Oh good, I thought I stepped over a boundary."

Ashley turns to her side and moves her back to the wall and straightens out her legs to lie across the booth. "No boundaries here. But I see the way he looks at you."

"There is nothing there."

"Hmmhmm," she says and yawns while she scoots herself out of the booth. "I better get back to work. I need to close. Thanks for letting me eat with you. We should hang out sometime. I need more girlfriends."

I follow her lead out of the booth. "We should. That would be fun. What's your number?"

We both exchange our numbers, and she pulls me into a quick hug. "See you later."

CHAPTER SIX

I'M SITTING HERE on the stool behind the antique register, waiting for the day to pick up. I don't think it will. After having dinner with Ashley, I've done more research and Googled this place. And she was right. It's a popular town. I feel like an idiot for not doing my research. Thinking straight wasn't a priority for me when I left. Who can think straight after being thrown like a rag doll?

The squeaky door and floorboard pull me out of my thoughts, and Ashley walks through with a bag in hand.

"Hey," she says and lays the bag down on the counter.

"Hey, what are you doing here?"

"I wanted to bring you lunch." She lifts a brown paper bag. "We had extra food made for the farmer's market, and Cruz doesn't like food to go to waste, so I brought it to you."

I pull the bag closer to me and peek inside. It looks like a hamburger wrapped up with a side of sweet potato fries. They know my order so well already. "What farmer's market?"

Ashley lifts herself onto the counter and sits. I check around to make sure June isn't present. I can already hear her bickering over it.

"There is a small farmer's market that local businesses do twice a year."

"Isn't it too hot right now?"

Ashley erupts in laughter. "Not for us locals. We're kind of used to it. We try to go early in the morning and late evening to avoid the sun."

How does anyone get used to this? "So Cruz Brewery makes burgers for people at the farmer's market? It seems like they would sell beer instead of food?"

"Ummm... well, this year, we decided to do food too," she says with a guilty look.

I shrug my shoulders, not thinking anything of it. "Okay. Thank you."

Ashley jumps off the counter. "I better get back to work. Come by when you're off. And wait for the sun to go down a little."

"Yeah, that sounds like fun. I'll be there."

"See you later." She heads out the door.

I hear June rattling on about something in the distance, and then I hear a loud bang. I rush toward the back and see she has dropped a box on the ground and notice she's cradling one of her hands in the other.

"Are you okay?"

"Yes, this damn arthritis in my hands. They lock up on me all the time."

I bend down and grab the box. "Where do you want the box?"

"Up front is fine." June follows behind me. "I guess it's time for another steroid shot," she says.

"My grandma gets steroid shots in her feet. She said it usually hurts for a few days after the shot. Does it do the same with your hands?" I grab some scissors and open the box.

"Yeah, it sucks getting old. So you have a grandma?"

I pull out what's in the box. So far it's a lot of '80s clothes. Who the hell is going to buy this? Maybe for Halloween? I always question the items despite random people buying them.

"Yup, and a grandpa, too," I say.

"How come you came down here?"

"I told you, for a fresh start."

"No one comes down to this town for a fresh start unless they're running from something."

I start hanging the clothes up on the clothing rack. "Not me." I grin to hide the fact that I am running from something—my past life.

June mumble something to herself, and then she asks me, "Do you have any parents?"

"Of course I do. How else would I have been born? My dad left when I was young, and my mom never got over it, so she wasn't the best mother. My grandparents raised me."

"Your grandparents don't care that you picked up and left?"

"They do. But they also trust me and my decisions." This is the most she has tried to have a conversation with me. She sticks to herself and doesn't seem like she wants to be bothered.

After about twenty minutes, I look around for June and find her in the back. "I finished hanging all the clothes. Do you need me to do anything else?"

"No. Why don't you head out of here, and I'll lock up."

"Are you sure?"

"Yes. Yes. Go," she says, waving her arms toward the door.

"Okay. I'll be upstairs if you need me." I grab the lunch Ashley brought and head up the stairs.

The sun is going down a little. At least it's not at the point in the sky where it beams straight down at you. Ashley had forgotten to tell me where the farmer's market was. I texted her, and she sent me the address. I throw on a pair of jean shorts, a black spaghetti strap, and white sneakers. Since it's walking distance, I thought it would be nice to take a walk.

It's been nice not having to drive everywhere. I hate driving. That's one thing I enjoyed about Chris; he always drove. Even if he didn't want to, he would anyway. I stop and hold my composure. He unexpectedly came to my mind and I can't believe it. I've been so busy I haven't had a chance to dwell on my anger and sadness. I push aside my feelings and head out.

I'm already dripping sweat, and I'm not even there yet. I'll have to get used to the heat if I want to start a new life here and not hibernate in my apartment with my swamp cooler. I never realized how nice they were for small spaces. It cools the studio down in no time. As I'm walking over there, I bypass a lot of the locals. They're all so friendly and say hi or wave at me. Are they wondering who I am? Since everyone else I start a conversation with questions my being here.

Twenty tents line the street up ahead. That must be the place. It's bigger than I thought it would be in a small town. There must be more family businesses that I don't know about. I make my way through the crowd and start scanning each tent. There are many homemade things like bread, pastries, and jewelry.

I stop at the bread that is being made right outside in a portable oven on wheels. Bread is my weakness.

"Hi, what can I get for you?" the lady asks.

"These all look so good. I can't choose."

"We are local. If you like what you get and want to try a different kind, you can get it at the local grocery store before you leave town."

"That's good to know. I just moved here. I'll have to stop by," I say with a side-eye to see if she makes some sort of expression.

"Oh, forgive me. I've never seen you around, so I thought you were a visitor."

I nod. "I'll take one pack of your sourdough bread for now, and then I'll make sure to stop by the grocery store and get more when I finish this one."

"Sounds like a plan."

She finishes ringing me up, and I head over to meet Ashley. The closer I get, the only person I see is Cruz and another guy.

"Hi," I say.

Cruz hurries and stands up. "Hey, how are you?"

I notice there is no food on the table, only beer on draft. "Did you sell out of your food already?"

Cruz's eyebrows squint. "We never had food. Only beer. Are you hungry? Ashley is working right now. You should stop by the brewery and get yourself some dinner."

"Oh. She's not here?" I say, rubbing my hand over my forehead.

He gives me a questionable look. "Did she say she would be here?"

"Yeah. She came by and dropped lunch off for me at the shop. She said you guys had made too much and didn't want it to go to waste." I cut myself off, finally understanding what she is doing. Cruz must know now, too, because he is holding back a smile by biting his lips. "I must have heard her wrong. I'll take beer to-go."

He nods, still trying to hold in his laugh. I watch as he pulls the lever down and fills a cup of beer for me.

He hands me the beer and asks, "How are you liking it here so far?"

"It's good. And hot. Really hot." I take a sip of the beer so it won't spill when I move.

A chuckle comes from him. "If you stay here long enough, you'll get used to it. Are you planning on staying here long?"

"I like it so far and don't have any plans to leave."

He's the only one so far who hasn't questioned why I decided to move here. I remember Ashley telling me he was born and raised here. He obviously isn't running from anything. Like everyone says this town is for.

"Cheers." He raises his cup to mine.

We both stand in silence, gazing at one another again. I hurry and break eye contact before he notices the grin that's forming. There is something about him that makes me shy. Maybe it's his looks? Or the look he gives me when I catch ourselves gazing at one another.

I turn back over to him once I know I can hold my composure. "I better get going."

"Okay, it was nice seeing you again." He smirks. "See you around, Tessa," he says, waving me off.

I back away, stumbling on my two feet after hearing him say my name in a sultry voice. Both of my cheeks feel hotter than normal. Is it from heat or his voice? At this rate, I can't tell.

After a few hours at the farmer's market, I'm back at my place, sitting on my bed and eating the bread I bought for dinner. I was too embarrassed to go to the brewery and see Ashley in case Cruz stopped by. This is the first time in days I'm sitting with my thoughts. Lately, I've been dead tired and knocked out the second I hit the bed.

My mind wanders to Chris, wondering what happened that night. Even though I'm angry, my chest constricts with an ache. My mind knows it was wrong, but my heart feels the hurt he's put me through. I never saw myself in an abusive relationship.

At least I left the first time he hit me. Some never leave. He blames me for something, and I don't know what it is. His eyes are something I can't stop seeing. Eyes I never imagined seeing again. But when you grow up with it, it sticks with you. No matter how hard you try to oversee it.

CHAPTER SEVEN

Ashley: What are you doing tonight?

Me: Nothing. already in bed.

Ashley: What! Get your ass up. We're all going night swimming.

Me: Who's we?

Ashley: Some friends. And Cruz will be there.

Me: You're not that slick anymore. I know what you're trying to do.

Ashley: What are you talking about? I've done nothing. Now put your swimsuit on and meet me in front of the shop in twenty.

Me: And if I say no?

Ashley: I'll drag your ass out.

Me: It's Saturday night, don't you have to work?

Ashley: You can't think Cruz is that cruel to me and not let me get some Saturdays off. Stop deflecting and let's go.

Me: Fine, I'll meet you in twenty.

I'M outside in my bikini and short shorts, looking like a hooker waiting for her bait, twenty minutes later. No point in covering up too much if I'll remove it later. Before going downstairs, I took two shots. As the new girl in town, I'm nervous to be around so many people. Because it's a small community, I'm sure word has spread that I'm either nuts about relocating here or running from something.

Ashley pulls around the corner in a black Mercedes and yells through her window, "Get in!"

I'm not sure how she manages to afford a black Mercedes. The brewery must offer a nice wage. I'm not one to pass judgment. I get in through the passenger door. Ashley reaches over as much as the seat allows her to and hugs me.

"How have you been? You haven't come by the brewery in days."

"I've been working and fixing up my place. June is letting me do whatever I want. It's pretty old, and no one has lived in it in years. There is a lot of work. Where's the pool we're headed to?"

"It's at Cruz's house." She pulls back onto the road. "He rarely lets anyone use it because he likes his privacy, but once in a while, he likes to have some people over."

"Are there going to be a lot of people?"

She shrugs. "Maybe five to ten people. Trust me, he's not all about huge-ass parties, especially if it's at his house."

We take a turn down a route I had no idea existed. The main street was the only visible street with a few blocks of houses. Ahead of us is a dim path lined with trees; the more we drive, the more light shines our way. We stop in front of a white rambler with a wraparound porch. Ashley parks the car, and we both exit. I follow Ashley's lead to the front entrance, where I notice a wooden swing hanging from the porch's roof.

"Cruz lives here?" I ask.

"Yup. It's cute, huh?" She helps herself and opens the front door.

"Very."

A warm apple scent fills my nostrils as I walk into the house. Passing the family room, it appears untouched. I'm sure owning a business doesn't leave him with much time to enjoy his own home. The kitchen is bright and open with many windows that shine the night sky in. There are all sorts of booze bottles and other finger foods on the island.

Ashley pours tequila into two different shot glasses. Then she reaches over, grabs two limes, and dips them in salt.

"Ready for a shot?" She hands me one of them.

We both cheers, shoot it down, and take a bite of the salted lime. There's a group in the pool, some I recognize from the bar.

"Do you want a beer to drink while in the pool?"

"Sure."

She hands me a beer. "Let's go."

I follow Ashley's lead outside and a smile forms on Cruz's face the second he sees me. I can't help but blush a little in response. We walk down the porch steps and head for the pool. Many trees surround the backyard just like the front of the house. The property is very secluded. Something that sounds perfect for Cruz.

"Hey, you came," Cruz says.

"Yes, I did. Thanks for inviting me." Both of my cheeks rise from my smile.

"Everyone, this is Tessa. Tessa, this is Jason, Caleb, and his girlfriend, Marnie."

Everyone looks over and says hi and waves. I wave back to them as I pull off my shorts and toss them next to the pool. I dip myself into the pool, getting used to the temperature of the water. The warm water doesn't take me long to adjust to. I'm not as nervous as I was before. This is pretty low-key and everyone seems friendly.

Out of the corner of my eye, I notice Cruz headed toward me. I give him a slight smile and say, "Your house is beautiful."

"Thanks. It was a long process to build it from the ground up," he says as we both admire the house.

"Did you build it yourself?" I turn my head in his direction and admire his five o'clock shadow that lies around his prominent jaw.

"Pretty much. The things I couldn't do, I hired help."

"When did you find time to build it? You must be pretty busy with the brewery."

He turns to me and catches me staring at him. A small smirk forms on his face when he notices. "That's why it took me a while to finish it."

Ashley cuts in, "Don't forget I helped you."

Cruz chuckles a little. "Yes, you did. And you never let me forget it. I don't know what I would have done without you."

I look over at Ashley and she flips her hair back with her eyebrows raised.

"Are you part owner, Ashley?"

"I should be," she says with a laugh. "Just kidding. I was always there when he needed me. Even on my days off. Even when I was out on a date." She gives Cruz a stern look. "I'm proud to have been there every step of the way."

Cruz reaches over and cheers Ashley.

"That's nice. You guys must be very close?" I ask.

"We are. We grew up together. She's like a little sister to me," Cruz says and gives her a little shove.

"Hey!" Ashley splashes his face.

More rounds of shots are taken throughout the night. I'm pretty woozy at this point and I'm getting an overwhelming feeling of the night I left Chris. I can't pinpoint what it is and where it's coming from. Everyone's having fun. The situation now is not like that night. Flashbacks keep coming back up. Unwelcome memories resurfaced. I worked so hard to keep my childhood memories at bay. Now here I am with the same memories, but now they're flashbacks of me, not my mom.

I've gotten quieter with the crowd and Cruz notices because he keeps looking over at me. Everyone has been so nice and including me in conversations. Conversation flowed all night. No one even questioned why I moved here. So why am I feeling like this? Cruz's eyes don't leave my sight. It's making me a little nervous because I don't want to get sensitive around everyone. I can tell by his glances toward me that he knows something is going on.

I turn around and head for the pool steps, and Ashley yells, "Hey, babe, where are you going?"

Trying to hide my tears from them, I keep my head facing the house and say, "I'll be right back. I'm going to the bathroom."

I quiver more when I step out of the water. Is my body finally recuperating from the trauma of that night? I climb up the porch steps and find someone's towel, which I wrap around myself.

As I walk into the house, another draft of cool air hits me and makes me shiver again. Once I find the bathroom, I check my reflection in the mirror as I walk in. My bloodshot eyes are watering. I splash water on my face, still attempting to keep back tears. I bite down on my lower lip, discovering it's numb. The booze has taken effect faster than I anticipated. I spin around and face the wall, attempting to maintain my cool. I didn't want to ruin the night because I couldn't control my drinking or emotions.

A knock comes on the door. "I'll be right out," I say.

On the other side of the door, I hear Cruz. "Is everything okay?"

Shit, I didn't want anyone to see me like this. My eyes are still glowing red. I could blame it on the chlorine and alcohol. I hurry and wipe my face off with the towel and open the door.

"Yes, I'm okay."

He stands there, examining my eyes. "Are you sure?"

I nod.

He reaches his hand up and gently touches my cheek. My body jolts back. He's surprised by my reaction and so am I. Trauma makes your body have a mind of its own. It's getting harder to control mine right now.

Cruz tilts his head to the side, making strong eye contact with me.

I look down at my feet, taking a few steps forward. "We should head back," I say as I bypass him, swiping my shoulder against his chest. He reaches down and grabs my hand. My body jumps in shock. I pull away from him faster than I realize because my head slams into the wall in front of the bathroom. Throbbing invades my head and the tears I was holding back spill out of me. I stand, head in hands, crying in front of a stranger.

"Can I get you anything?" he asks.

All I want to do is go home, despite shaking my head. Cruz steps a little closer to me. I lift my head and face him. The dizziness hits me harder. Through my tears and alcohol, I squint to see him clearly.

"Stay right here." He walks off into another room.

Examining my head through the mirror in the bathroom, I don't see a bump. Hopefully, one doesn't form tomorrow.

"Here," Cruz says, handing me a pair of sweats and a sweater. "Put these on. I'm going to tell everyone I'm taking you home. I'll be right back."

He turns his back to me and heads out. Without even thinking about drying myself off more, I put on the clothes he gave me. Their warmth helps calm me down a little. A warm scent lingers on them and I inhale the smell.

"Are you ready?" Cruz says, standing at the doorway with keys in his hands.

I remain silent as I gaze up at him. We both start heading out.

The entire drive home, I was silent and so was he. I hope he doesn't make this bigger than it is. He seems to respect my boundaries because he hasn't asked any questions. Cruz puts his truck in park. "Can I walk you up so I know you got in okay?"

"You don't have to. I feel bad enough for ruining your night."

"You didn't ruin my night. I had fun."

"I'm sure you didn't expect all this," I say as I turn to face him. Since we got into the truck, I haven't looked at him once.

"I own a brewery. I've seen a lot of crazy shit. This is nothing," he says with a wink. "But I would feel better if I walked you to your door."

"Okay." I tug on the door handle and slide out of his truck. Once I reach the steps, he waits for me to go first.

We both reach the door and I flip on the light to my place. I wish I had cleaned up a little. I have shit everywhere from trying to clean the place and paint. "It's messy. I've been redoing the place."

He stands in the doorway with his eyes on me. His sweet grin warms my face a little.

"I better let you get to sleep. If you ever need anything, I'm always here."

"Thank you. And thank you for everything. I had a lot of fun."

He gives me one nod, turns his back to me, and I watch as he heads down the stairs.

CHAPTER EIGHT

Tessa

TODAY HAS BEEN busy at the shop, giving me no time to think about the past weekend. I haven't talked to Cruz or Ashley since then. I didn't say goodbye, so I'm not sure what everyone thought. Updating the studio has been keeping my mind busy, not dwelling on anything.

"Hi, can I help you look for anything?" I ask what I'm assuming is a mother and her teenage daughter.

"Are these your only '80s clothes?" the daughter asks.

"For right now, yes. We're always getting new pieces in. I assume you're visiting?"

"We are," the mother says.

"Mom, let's dress up like the '80s for Halloween." The daughter pulls the bell-bottom pants up to her waist and looks down at them.

"Oh, honey, that's what I grew up wearing," she says with a grin on her face.

"It's perfect then. You'll be able to style us."

The mother erupts in a burst of laughter. "Fine."

The creaks from the front door distract me from watching the mother and daughter interaction. I glance over my shoulder and see Cruz walking in.

"I'll be over here if you guys need any help with anything," I say, pointing to the register.

They both glance my way and then turn their back toward me and continue looking at the clothes.

"Hey, what are you doing here?"

"I wanted to bring you some lunch and see how you were doing." He lifts a bag.

How thoughtful, but what's with him and Ashley always wanting to feed me? Don't get me wrong, I enjoy the food and the thought. Do they do this to anyone else? "You didn't have to do that."

"It's no problem. Remember, I own the food."

I laugh. "That's right."

"How have you been?" he says, standing in front of me with a soft grin on his face.

"Good. Listen, thanks for taking care of me that night or trying to. I know I was acting strange. The alcohol got to me."

"Nothing was strange. I wanted to make sure you were okay." He looks away from me. "I wanted to ask you something."

"Do you have a dressing room we could use?" I hear the daughter yell over to me, interrupting Cruz.

"Sorry. Hold on," I say to Cruz and walk over to them and open up the dressing room. "Here you go. Feel free to leave any unwanted items in the dressing room."

Cruz is leaning against the counter, watching me walk back over to him. My face heats up. This happens every time he's around. Does he notice?

"What were you saying?"

"I need to get wine from a winery a few hours away. I wanted to invite you. Would you want to get away for a little?" he says with a bashful smile.

"You're inviting me to a weekend getaway before taking me out on a date first?"

His eyebrows rise in shock like he didn't think this situation through. "Are you asking me out on a date?"

And now my eyebrows rise, not thinking before I blurted that out. "I mean, if you want to. It might be best before I go on a weekend getaway with you to make sure you're not a murderer." Oh geez, why can't I shut up?

"A murderer?"

"For all I know, you might be the town murderer."

He laughs. "Okay, let's go for dinner so I can prove to you I'm not the town murderer. I'll pick you up tonight at eight."

"See you at eight." Both my cheeks rise as I watch his broad shoulders turn around and walk out.

It's seven o'clock and I'm not sure what to wear. I'm having second thoughts about dating. I'm not ready to start dating. The other night, I made a mess at his house. Maybe it isn't a date. He might just be trying to do something nice by taking me out of town. Did I turn this into a date?

I sigh, looking at the mess on my bed. I have clothes thrown all over the place. A little mess can make this small space look like a tornado hit it. I've tried on everything I own and nothing looks good. I don't know where he's taking me, so I'm not sure how to dress. Are there any fancy restaurants here? I should've asked him.

After circling the room a million times, I find my phone

under a pile of clothes. How the hell did it get here? Opening up my contact list, I realize I don't have his number. I let out another agonizing sigh. I need to stop overthinking this and calm the hell down. Ashley runs through my mind. God, why didn't I think to text her?

> Me: Ashley! Emergency!

Falling back down onto my bed, I hope she replies soon. I only have forty-five minutes now. My phone rings, bringing me up from my bed. "Ashley."

"Are you okay? What happened?"

Oh shit, I shouldn't have made it sound like it was an actual emergency. "I'm going on a date and I need help choosing what to wear."

"You bitch. Don't scare me like that."

"Sorry," I mumble.

"What time is your date?"

"Umm." I look down at my phone. "In forty-four minutes."

"I'll be there in ten." She hangs up.

Ten minutes later, I hear a knock on my door. "Coming," I yell.

Before I can get the door open all the way, Ashley barges in with clothes wrapped around her arms. She throws them on the bed, turns back around, and looks at me. "I brought so many options that will look good on your body frame."

"My body frame?"

"Yes. You're very petite, but you fill out every angle of your body well."

"I don't know where we're going, so I don't know how to dress."

She pulls out a blank spaghetti strap dress. "This one. Try this one on."

I pull it away from her. "Did you hear me? I don't know

where we're going. What if this is too fancy?" I say, examining the dress.

"This won't be too fancy," she says as she undresses me.

"How do you know?" Despite not knowing each other for long, she undresses me as if we've known each other our whole lives. She makes it easy to be comfortable around.

"I called Cruz before I came over here and he told me where he was taking you."

"What! How'd you know the date was with Cruz?"

She pulls the dress down my body, straightening it as she works her way back up. I look down at myself. The dress fits me nicely. It's the right amount of length. It stops mid-thigh, not too tight and not too flowy. I turn around and look at myself in the mirror. "Wow, Ashley. You have good taste. I love it." It's a slight V-neck, making my boobs pop out a little, but not showing too much.

"Here, try these on?" She hands me a pair of black high heels with thin laces that wrap around the foot up to the ankles.

After getting the heels on, I stand up and stare at myself in the mirror. Shocked at what I see, I'm at a loss for words. It's been a while since I've dressed up and I forgot how good I could look. "You still haven't answered my question. How'd you know my date was with Cruz?"

She fixes the curls in my hair. "Who else would you be going with?"

My eyes narrow toward her.

"What? I see the way you guys look at each other."

"What do you mean?"

"Come on. His face lights up every time you enter the room and your cheeks turn red every time you see him."

"They do not." I already know they do, but I don't want to admit it.

"They do. Your cheeks are turning red right now just by talking about him."

I reach up and touch my cheeks with both of my hands. They are a little warm, but I didn't think it was noticeable. Ashley slaps my hands away from my face. "Don't touch. You're going to ruin your makeup."

"You flat out asked Cruz if it was me he was going on a date with and he told you just like that?"

"I told you. We're close. He tells me everything." Ashley walks over to her purse and pulls something out of it. "Pout your lips so I can put lipstick on you."

"Are you sure you guys haven't ever had a thing together because you know sometimes best friends turn into something more?"

"Shut up and pout your lips."

I do as I'm told and pout my lips.

"And no. We've never been and never will be anything more. And ew for thinking that."

"What? It's an honest question."

"Trust me. He sees me as a bro and I see him as a girlfriend."

"So then, where are we going? I've never seen any fancy places around here."

She turns around and places her lipstick back in her purse. "There are more places outside of the one Main Street, you see. You have to explore and find them. He's taking you to this fancy wine bar called Cliffs Wine Bar."

A knock comes on my door and we both turn toward it. I turn back to face her, eyes wide with flutters in my stomach.

"Your face is doing it again."

I reach up and touch my cheeks. Oh, no. They're warm. I try to cool them down by waving both of my hands up and down. I take a deep breath and exhale.

She spins me back around, facing the door. "Okay, go, go, go and have a good time." She spanks my ass.

His eyes light up the second he sees me. "Wow, you look beautiful." He hands me a bouquet of pink and white daisies.

"Thank you." I take the flowers from his grasp. "Let me set these down real quick."

"I'll take them," Ashley says in the background.

I face my back toward Cruz and narrow my eyebrows at her. "He's not supposed to know you're here," I whisper.

"He already knew."

My face drops. Now he's going to know she dressed me.

CHAPTER NINE

Tessa

NEITHER OF US spoke during the drive to the restaurant. He seems nervous just like me. I'm not sure how long it's been since he last dated. Ashley mentioned he doesn't date much or with locals.

The restaurant's atmosphere is very romantic. The lights are dimmed with a candle glowing light in the middle of the tables. It's a very calming place. Many couples are around enjoying their time. Every time I look over at the couple in front of me, I notice the girl's cheeks glow a rosy pink shade as she tilts her head, giving off a bashful, cutesy look.

"How do you like your wine?" he asks.

"It's good. I've never been much of a wine drinker. It's nice adventuring out." The waiter suggested I get a flight of wine with a mix of reds and whites so I could sample each and decide which I preferred.

"Have you been here before?" I ask Cruz.

"A few times."

A nod slightly. Should I have asked that? It might have been with another girl.

"With my mom. This is her favorite place."

He must have seen my questioning look.

"Oh, that's nice of you," I say with a smile. Taking his mom out to a place like this makes it seem like he treats her well. You know what they say. If the man treats their mother right, he'll treat you right. After saying that in my head, Chris comes to mind. He treated his mom right. The saying may not always be true. But then again, that burning in his eyes only told me one thing. Cruz interrupts my thoughts while he clears his voice. I look up at him and ask, "Are you and your mom close?"

"Yeah. It's been me and her for a long time. My dad passed away when I was a teenager."

"Sorry to hear about your dad."

He shrugs. "Shit happens. My parents didn't have the greatest relationship. Not saying he should have died. They shouldn't have stayed together as long as they did."

"That's rough." I empathize. "I was raised by a shitty mother for a while, so I understand how you feel."

"Is your dad still in the picture?"

"No. He walked out on my mom and me when I was a toddler. Not sure why. My mom won't ever talk about it when I ask. I think she blamed me for him walking out."

"Did she tell you it was your fault?"

"No. But as a child, you have the sixth sense of being blamed for something, but since you're young, they never come out and say it."

The waiter comes by and sets down a charcuterie board. "Thank you, Susan," Cruz says.

"Do you know everyone here?" I ask as I pick up a piece of

toasted bread and spread meat and cheese on it. It's one of those restaurants that serve you slowly to make sure you finish each course first. I try not to eat too much of the appetizer before my main course because I don't finish it. I can't keep my hunger at bay because I haven't eaten since noon, and I'm hungry.

"Pretty much. You know everyone if you're born and raised here. Do you have any siblings?"

"Nope, just me. My grandparents took me in and raised me after I turned twelve."

"We kind of have a similar background," Cruz says.

Not really, I think. *I doubt your mom was in and out of abusive relationships. Doing any drug the next runner-up offered her.* She wanted to be loved so badly by someone after my dad left her. She'd do anything to keep them, even if it meant them laying their hands on her. That wasn't the worst of it. She suddenly started hanging out with the wrong crowd, and that led to dating drug addicts. As a result, she became addicted to drugs. The things she did for love. And that is not even actual love. At least it shouldn't be.

I remember the PTSD I got every time a new guy worked his way into our house. Never knowing what this one was going to do. It all turned out the same, though. At first, they were always giddy, like two little kids on a playground. Until real-life adult shit came around and then they had to deal with it. Instead of dealing with it, they turned to drugs, which led to abuse.

For a long time, my grandparents were clueless. With each passing year, my mom's appearance diminished. Then my grandparents were always questioning what was happening. The more she lied, the more questions came. When that happened, I saw less and less of them. After a while, they became aware of what was happening. Police would periodically show up at our door for a welfare check. My mom played them so well that they never questioned anything. She never kept the drugs lying out in case I got to them. At least she thought that far ahead. That's what helped her not get questioned by the police. That, and I would lie to them and say everything was fine. She never realized her hold on me. I always dreamed of her getting better and we'd have a mother-and-daughter relationship. I couldn't have that if they took her away, so I lied.

After watching the same cycle time and time again, I knew she wouldn't get better. It was like clockwork never missed a second of it. When I had enough, I ran away to my grandparents and told them everything. They took my mom to court to get custody of me and the rest is history because they won. I wasn't sure how they won so easily because my mom never got caught by the police with drugs. She never called the police anytime a lowlife laid a hand on her. How did they know her history? The older I got, the more questions I had, and that's when everything pieced together. There were times she wouldn't come home for an entire weekend. Sometimes even a week. I thought she was out vacationing. Turns out she was in jail all those times. That's what taught me how to take care of myself. I made it a mission to take care of myself, so I didn't have to call my grandparents. We knew they were the ones who would call the police to our house. And if I wanted that relationship with my mom, I couldn't tell anyone.

Soon after, I left my mom's house for good. Calls came sporadically. Until there were none. I couldn't even tell you where she went. She left her house and daughter behind. We had no number to reach her on. After years of tolerating her, I had to make peace with it all. We couldn't have a relationship because she was sick. My grandparents filled that void, so it wasn't hard.

"Um, yeah, if you say so."

"I'm sorry. I didn't mean anything by it. I only meant that we didn't grow up with the conventional picket fence with both parents to come home to."

"It's okay. I thought nothing of it," I say.

A sizzling noise catches us both off guard. Susan sets down

our steaks that are lying on a hot plate. Then she places the lobster mac and cheese in the middle of the table. We both start digging in. Seems like he's hungry just as much as I am.

"How long have you had your brewery open?"

"Five years."

"Wow. It's going well. Was it hard starting your own business?" We both reach over for the mac and cheese, bumping our hands together, sending a static spark between us. "That was weird," I say as I rub my hands together to release the pin and needle feeling that came afterward.

Cruz smiles. "Go ahead and serve. Ladies first."

"Thanks."

"Yes, to your question. Starting a business was hard. Running it was even harder. Once you get the right employees, everything falls into place."

"Your mom must be very proud," I say.

"Would you guys like some more wine?" Susan asks, holding up the wine bottle.

I shake my head. "I'm okay." I'm already tipsy. The last thing I want is a reenactment of the other night.

Susan tops off Cruz's wine, smiles at us, and walks away.

"Were your grandparents okay with you coming here all by yourself?"

My eyes go wide. That question caught me off guard. After all the conversations we have had, he's never questioned me coming here. Never gave me the crazy look everyone else has given me. That's what drew me to him.

"Yes, they were okay with it." That's all I can think to say. I don't want to go into too much detail about my coming here. He must notice because he changes the subject.

"How do you like it so far?"

"I like it so far. It hasn't been bad. Everyone has been welcoming."

"That's good. You think you will stay long?"

"I have no plans to leave yet. If that answers your question."

A big grin rises from his lips, causing my cheeks to heat. Not again. I reach over and grab the cup of water to cool myself down. Do my cheeks look like the cutesy girl's in front me? I hope the darkness of the restaurant hides my cheeks, but I doubt it since I can see the other girl's.

After dinner, Cruz walks me to the passenger side of his truck and opens the door for me. It's a little awkward. This is new to me. It's a five-minute drive back to my place. "Thank you for dinner. It was delicious." I watch Cruz get into the truck and drive off.

"I'm glad you liked it."

"Now I know why that's your mom's favorite place." I chuckle.

"I'll have to tell her you like it, too."

"Does she know about me?"

"She knows I had dinner with someone. She's the one who recommended this place."

Silence fills the truck. I'm surprised again. He already spoke to his mom about our date. Was this even a date? Wait, he said dinner. Before, he mentioned wanting to take me out over the weekend to get away. I brought up the date as a joke. I have this all wrong. Even Ashley said he doesn't date. Cruz pulls up to my place and puts the truck in park. I slide out of the truck after opening the door. Once my feet hit the ground, I see Cruz right in front of me.

"I was coming to open the door for you," he says.

"Oh. I got it." I head toward the stairs and Cruz follows behind me, keeping the silence as I walk up the stairs.

"Well, this is me." I unlock the door. I'm unsure of how to end the night. This is getting awkward. We're now facing each other. Cruz has a look of wanting to speak but remains silent. He moves a little closer to me and wraps his arms around me. I stand there, shocked, and wrap my hand around him. We let go of each other. He turns his back to me and heads down the stairs.

"I'll see you later. Have a good night," he says over his shoulder

"Good night."

CHAPTER TEN

Cruz

IT'S HUMBLING to wash dishes at your brewery again after years of delegating it to staff. My dishwasher called in sick, and instead of asking someone else to cover him, I'm doing it myself. It's good to humble yourself now and then and know what you had to do to get started. Everyone who keeps coming in and out of the kitchen and sees me doing the dishes gives me a questionable look. I ignore them altogether. For the past few days, I've been in a good mood. I'm not always in a bad mood, but I'm in a better mood now and I know why. That one girl who caught my eye the moment she slid in front of me on my brewery bar stool. The constant eye contact didn't help my questioning, either.

Ashley has joined me, sitting on the counter next to me. She has this mysterious smile on her face and I raise my eyebrows to see what she wants. "Can I help you?"

Her smile gets bigger, like she's excited about something.

I stare her dead in the eyes. "Well?"

She rolls her eyes. "Come on, Cruz. You know what I'm here for."

"No. I really don't," I mutter. "Don't you have work to do?"

"Yes, but you know I won't leave until all my work is complete." She sways her legs back and forth with a giddy smile.

"So then why aren't you working?" I ask.

"Do I have to spell it out?" she says sarcastically.

"Obviously, because I don't know what you are waiting for me to say." I turn back over and continue washing the dishes.

She shoves my shoulder. "Don't play dumb. How was your date?"

"Oh, that. It was good."

"That's all you're going to say?" She grabs my shoulders, trying to turn me toward her.

I lean my waist against the sink, set the rag down, and look at her with my arms crossed. "I thought we had a good time together. I did anyway. But at the end of the night, she seemed a little standoffish. I hugged her and told her to have a good night. She seemed a little uneasy about it. Maybe she doesn't enjoy being touched."

"Maybe she doesn't, because she didn't seem to like your touch that night at your house."

"You better not have told her I told you."

"Come on, you know I keep my secrets."

"That would be hard for me if she doesn't like touch. Because I have to have touch in a relationship," I whisper as one of my employees is walking right at me.

"Hey, boss?" I look over at Jason calling my name. "It's slowing down out there. Is it all right if I order something?"

"Yes, go ahead," I say.

Jason turns his back toward us, stops, and looks back over. "How's Tessa?"

I give him a dead stare, confused. "Good. Why?" No one saw

her that night. I told them she was getting tired and wanted to go home. I can tell she's a private person. The last thing I wanted to do was say anything.

"Just curious. I like her," he says, turns back around, and heads toward the bar. "For you." I hear him say in the distance.

Ashley shoves my shoulder again. "See."

I start on the dishes again, ignoring everyone. People seem to forget I'm a grown man. I know where my feelings are headed. I don't need anyone directing them for me.

"Anyway, how do you know you like touch if you haven't been with someone in a while?" Ashley asks.

My eyes go wide. "Could you say it any louder? You know I don't like people to know my business."

"Sorry," she whispers.

"You act like I've never dated."

"I don't even remember the last time you had a relationship."

"It doesn't matter. I know what I want."

"Okay, okay, geez," she says, raising her hands like she's been caught red-handed. "What's your theory on why she ran away?"

"I don't know. But it doesn't matter."

"I'm just saying... It might be part of why she doesn't enjoy being touched. I think she thought it was a date. There is a mutual attraction between you two, and she's not clueless. You even invited her for a weekend getaway to Colorado. Speaking of that, are you still taking her?"

Maybe I'm moving too fast. Women throw themselves at me, and I hated that. They made it too easy. And they can easily move on to the next guy. I backed away altogether. Except for the occasional one-night stands. I picked tourists to steer clear of emotional connections. *Fuck,* that makes me sound like a douchebag. I've been out of the game for too long. She has a certain mystique that draws me in. She always smiles, despite her shy and mysterious look. But those eyes told a different story at my house that night. I'm unsure of what it is. I know she hides something dark from her past. Something about it makes me curious, but I don't want to be nosy.

"I'm still planning on taking her."

Ashley jumps off the counter. "Good. I think it's a good idea," she says as she walks away.

CHAPTER ELEVEN

I'M SITTING OUTSIDE, watching the sunset in front of my door. I have very limited space here, from the stairs up to my place to the entrance, but I have enough to set a chair out and watch the night sky fall most nights after dinner. When I can't sleep, I come out to look at the moon. It comforts me knowing I'm not alone, like the sun and the moon are watching over me. It's been a while since I've been alone. The only time I was alone in a house was when my mom would leave for weeks.

I appreciate the stuff I went through with my mom because it made me strong. Sometimes I yearn for someone else to save me and catch me when I fall. I've always been the one to save myself. Chris wasn't a bad guy when we met. He was nice, funny, and charming. He charmed everyone he met. I fell fast for him, and we moved in together even faster. That was my first mistake, moving in with him before knowing him. But do you ever really know someone fully? That night, I felt like my mom.

You can be the strongest person, but the strongest can sometimes fail, too. I didn't want to be that person. I left to keep myself safe so I wouldn't drown in the same cycle I've watched repeatedly.

My mind constantly goes back to that night. Did I miss something? Was this behavior in front of me? Was I too head over heels to see it? The last year keeps replaying in my mind like a broken record. Growing up, I learned the signs. Even though I knew the signs, why was I unable to see this coming? Chris kept saying it was my fault. My fault for what? There was no use in questioning him. When someone is in that state of mind, nothing gets past what they think and know. Half the time, what they think and know isn't reality.

I notice lights pulling up into the parking lot in front of me. A truck. Butterflies swarm my stomach. *Cruz.*

I feel drawn to him. Not sure what it is. I had no desire to start something. But something is there that connects us deeper than I can explain. *Damn it*, heat rises in my cheeks again.

"What are you doing outside all alone?" He walks up the stairs and takes a seat on the top step.

"I live alone. Whether I'm inside or outside, I'm still alone."

"Do you enjoy living alone?"

"I've done it before when I was younger." I cut myself off. There is something about him. I feel like I can be upfront and honest with him. But I always stop myself. I don't want to be known for my past. I want to start fresh and put everything else behind me. "What are you doing?"

"I just got done working. I wanted to stop by and see if you still wanted to go with me this weekend?"

As I glance at my phone, I realize it's almost midnight. I've been out here for a few hours now, lost in my thoughts. "Yes. I was still planning on it. Unless you don't want me to go anymore?"

"I do. I wasn't sure if you still wanted to go."

"Why wouldn't I?"

He looks out over the parking lot. "You have a good view here. No wonder you come out here."

"It is a nice view. I watch the sunset over the red rocks most nights. It helps me not feel so alone."

"I get that. It's nice living alone, but it can get too lonely sometimes."

"Have you always lived alone?" I ask as we both look at one another. The moon's reflection shines through his eyes, making it difficult not to become lost in them.

"Yup. Other than when I was growing up, living with my mom."

"You and Ashley never wanted to live together?"

"Hell no. I love her like a sister and that is it. Sometimes blood relatives don't enjoy living with each other. I've always liked living alone. I've never shared my space and never wanted to know what it's like."

"I guess growing up as an only child does that to you."

Cruz stands up and looks down at me. "I better get going. We leave tomorrow morning."

I sit up a little straighter. "Where is this place again? All I know is you could be dropping me off into a cult."

He rubs his hands through his hair and shakes his head. "I thought the date we went on was to prove I wasn't a murderer. Now I have to prove I'm not into some cult."

"I'm just kidding," I say. "What time will you be here to pick me up?"

"I'll be here at eight. That should give us enough time to get there before noon. It's a little winery from here called Palisade."

I stand up and reach over to hug him. At first, he's hesitant, and then he reciprocates and reaches in. "I'll see you in the morning," I say.

Me: Help!

Ashley: Is this an actual cry for help this time?
I don't trust you.

Me: What do I wear to a winery called
Palisade?

Ashley: I'll be over soon. I just got done at the
brewery.

Suddenly, I don't know how to dress myself. Like I lost touch with myself in this new town. I'm surprised when my front door swings open. Ashley stands there with a six-pack of beer in one hand and a brown bag in the other. My hands go to my chest, trying to catch my breath.

"What's wrong with you?" She stares at me with both of her eyebrows squinted together.

"You scared me."

"I told you I was coming over." She walks over to my kitchenette and sets down the bag and puts the beer in the fridge.

"I didn't expect you to storm in like that."

She pops open two beers and hands me one. "Here, I come bearing gifts."

I reach out for the beer and take a big chug. "What's in the bag?"

"Garlic fries. I haven't eaten and the only thing that sounded good were fries. So let's see your wardrobe."

I gesture toward the small door, which looks like a coat closet.

She walks over and opens it. "Is this all you own?"

"Yes."

"You poor thing." She shakes her head. "We need to take you shopping."

I slump down onto my bed. "Will anything I have work? Aren't wineries fancy?"

"Not this one. It's not like a high-end fancy one. Shorts and cute tank tops will do."

"Oh. Then I guess I didn't need you. I should have asked over the phone."

"Is this all our friendship is? You use me when you want me?" she says, riffling through my clothes.

"Shut up. You know it's not." I lie down on my bed just as Ashley comes over and lies right next to me. "Does Cruz talk to you about me?"

Silence.

"Your silence tells me he does," I say.

"Come on. You can't do this to me. I don't go around telling everything someone says to me. Obviously, he has talked about you or I wouldn't be trying to push you guys together."

"Why are you pushing us together?"

Ashley sits up and looks down at me. "Do you not want me to?"

"I'm just wondering what made you want us to be together?"

"He's a nice guy. I think he wants someone too. He won't come out and say it. There is something different about you that I thought would connect you two together."

"Like what?" I give her a puzzled look.

She gets up off the bed. "You're both so private and both don't want anyone in your business. You give a little but hold a lot in. You two are similar in that way. Who knows, you two might be each other's person that you tell your secrets to."

I sit up from the bed, watching her walk away. "Aren't you and Cruz close? Doesn't he tell you all his secrets?"

Ashley grabs the bag of fries, comes back over, and sits with her legs crossed over one another on the bed. "I know a lot about Cruz, but when I say he's private, he is private. He only shares what he wants to share. Everyone has their secrets. Some tell them to others and some don't. I wait for Cruz to say what he needs to. I obviously will ask questions, but I know him too well to know when he is going to tell me and when he's not."

"What secrets do you think I have?"

Ashley looks me dead in the eye. "Coming here alone tells a story. You either can share it or not. It's up to you. Either way, someone's story doesn't define them. I've never been one to complain if my friends tell me or not."

"What are your secrets?" I ask.

"You want to know?"

"No. I guess not. You can tell me when you want to. I don't want to pry into your life." I get up from the bed and head over to my closet. "I better start packing."

CHAPTER TWELVE

A TINY NUDGE against my shoulders jolts me out of my sleep. My eyes squint open, and I see green trees before me.

"We're here."

I rise from my seat and look around. It feels like no time has passed since I left early this morning with Cruz. "I slept the whole way over here?" I say, still hazy from sleeping. Ashley and I stayed up all night talking and the next thing we knew, the sun was coming out. We only slept a couple of hours before Cruz came to pick me up. Well, I only slept a couple of hours. I left Ashley sleeping before her noon shift at work.

"Yes, you did," he says as he puts the truck in park.

"Oh God. I'm sorry. You were probably so bored."

"I always come down here alone anyway. It was no different."

I chuckle. "I shouldn't have stayed up all night with Ashley."

"If you're still tired, you can go back to sleep in your room."

"No, I don't want to be boring. Let's go." I open the door and slide out to the ground. We're staying at a bed-and-breakfast called Country Inn. The place is a cute beige house. Cruz said he got us separate rooms. A lot of nerves left my body when he told me that. We walk up the steps and enter. On both sides of us, there are sitting areas with couches and tables. There's a hallway to the left and a stairway to the right.

"Hi, are you guys checking in?" a lady asks us.

"Yes, the reservations are under Cruz Bennet."

The lady scrolls through her iPad. "Follow me. I'll show you to your room."

All three of us walk up the steps that look rickety but are pretty sturdy. I think they aged the appearance for the place's aesthetic. She walks us down the very end of the hallway and opens the room. Cruz and I walk in first with her behind us. Cruz sets down my bag and turns and faces me.

"Does this look okay to you?"

It's your normal-looking hotel room with a bed, dresser, and table. I notice a balcony and walk over to it and look out. It's surprisingly green here compared to the dead surroundings on the way up. "Yes, it looks great."

"Where is the other room?" Cruz asks the lady.

She squints her eyebrows and looks down at her iPad. "It shows only one room under your name. Cruz Bennet, right?"

"Yes."

"Only one room is reserved under your name."

"I requested two rooms for the reservation."

"It says here that you canceled the other room. Leaving only one." She walks over to Cruz and points to her iPad. "See."

"There must be a mistake. I never canceled the other room."

"It says you canceled it a couple of days ago. I'm sorry, sir." She is still pointing to her iPad.

The only person who runs through my mind is *Ashley*. She's the only one I can see canceling the other room on purpose.

Cruz takes a few steps back and runs his hands through his hair. "That's okay. Can I get another room?"

"We're actually all booked out for the weekend?"

"Are you serious? The room was canceled a few days ago."

"Cruz, it's fine. I'm sure we'll manage," I say.

He turns toward me and nods. "It's fine. Thank you for your help," he says to the lady. Cruz shuts the door after she leaves. "I'm sorry. I got two rooms because I wanted to respect your privacy. I didn't cancel the other room. I'm not sure what happened."

"Ashley is what happened," I say.

"You're probably right." He rolls his eyes. "I'm going to kill her. I can look for another hotel." He pulls out his phone and starts typing.

I reach for his phone to stop him. "Hey, it's fine. I would rather explore the winery and not waste our time finding a place to sleep since we leave tomorrow."

"Are you sure? I don't want you to feel uncomfortable."

"Yes, stop worrying."

A man on a bicycle with a straw basket adds to this winery experience. There was a guy outside the first winery we stopped at renting out cruiser bicycles for people to ride around to each stop. There are about twenty stops. We won't be able to visit all the stops if we take these. But this seemed too fun to pass up.

I giggle as I watch Cruz jump off the bike. He gets off, pulls out his wedgy, and rearranges his pants. He gives me a side-eye and starts walking into the building. "I'm glad this is funny to you."

"You look so cute."

"I'm sure I do. I can't believe I let you talk me into this. A six-foot man cruising on this tiny bicycle. I'm surprised the tires held me up."

I let out a laugh as he explains himself on the bike. As we walk in, I notice a small group huddled together, sipping on wine while the guys give a little spiel about it. I'd like to visit as many stops as possible. Cruz said you're free to try the wine at each stop without having to talk about every single one. Unless you have questions.

We head to the far end of the counter. A guy is already pouring us a few samples of wine.

"Thank you," I say.

"If you have any questions, let me know," he says.

I'm looking at all the cheeses they have in the glass displays. There are a lot of pre-made charcuterie boards. I reach over and grab a sample of the Parmigiano Reggiano cheese they have out as samples.

"Do you like cheese?" Cruz asks.

"Yes. I used to make charcuterie boards for myself, but they never looked as fancy as the ones you order from the restaurant."

"Do you want to get one?"

"Maybe later. The cheese might melt with us riding around on our cute bicycles." I giggle. I look up at Cruz and he rolls his eyes at me.

A few hours have passed and every stop we make is making it harder to get back on our bicycles and ride to the next stop. I guess bike riding and alcohol don't go hand in hand that well. We're both getting pretty drunk and decide to stop for food. We pull our bikes up to one of the breweries that was suggested to us by the guy we rented the bikes from.

My ears fill with the sound of country music as we walk in, coming from the jukebox in the corner. We're not the only ones looking worn out. Many people are slumped over in their chairs, drinking water. They must have had the same idea as us. We take our seats at a booth, sitting across from each other. The waiter comes by and we both order water even though the waiter kept offering their house beer.

"So have I shown you enough that I'm not a murderer?"

I chuckle a little. "I wouldn't have come with you if I thought you were."

"Well, then I'm glad we got that straightened out." He winks.

I watch a few couples get up and dance to "Come a Little Closer" by Dierks Bentley. Both of my cheeks rise into a smile. I didn't notice Cruz had gotten out of his seat. Standing before me, he offers his hand. I look up at him, squinting my eyebrows. What is he doing?

"Let's dance."

"Oh no. I don't know how."

"Come on, everyone knows how to dance to slow music. All you do is sway your body to the music," he says.

"I'm too shy."

"Who is here to be shy around? No one knows us here."

I roll my eyes at him and place my hand in his. He helps me up from the booth and we both start walking to the dance floor. I wrap both of my arms around his neck and he circles my midsection. He's a lot taller than me, so it's hard to see over his shoulders. An older man comes by and pushes us closer together. With a big smile, he gives us a thumbs-up. Both of us chuckle. Cruz pulls me in a little closer and wraps his arms tighter. I rest the side of my head onto his chest as we both sway to the music.

This feels easy with him. We haven't had to try so hard to form a connection. I feel like this is where I belong. My body loosens up and settles a little more into his hold. His broad chest makes me feel safe. A safety I haven't felt my whole life. My exes never made me feel this way. Cruz barely knows me and he seems to care a lot for me. Cruz plants a kiss on the top of my head.

My eyes go blurry with the wetness of my tears. I'm trying

hard to hold them in and one slides down my cheek, soaking into Cruz's shirt. I don't know why all my emotions are coming out. Is it the alcohol? Or is it the fact that I never thought I could find someone who could be so gentle? I know there are men out there like that. For some reason, I never thought I would find one. Even if this doesn't go anywhere, his sweetness gives me a bit of hope.

The song has ended, and the four minutes that passed by felt like an eternity. But a good eternity. Like five years have passed by between me and Cruz, and I know him better. I feel safe around him. He releases me from his hold, and I hurry and wipe my eyes, hiding the wetness from them.

CHAPTER THIRTEEN

Tessa

"SORRY ABOUT MY HUSBAND." An older lady comes by our table with a beer in her hand. "He sometimes thinks he's a relationship counselor or something."

When I look over at her, I notice the man who pulled us together on the dance floor approaching us from behind.

"Ohhh, there's the lovely couple," he says.

Cruz's face turns upward, smiling at the couple.

"Honey, you can't always help yourself in people's relationships," the lady says.

"That's nonsense. They are a good-looking couple. A good-looking couple should be closer."

The lady pats his shoulders and rolls her eyes at him.

"Thank you for doing that. It did bring me closer to her," Cruz says with a wink.

The man's eyebrows rise and his eyes light up. "See."

A chuckle arises from me. "I'm Tessa and this is Cruz." I point over to Cruz, who reaches over to shake the man's hand.

"Nice to meet you. I'm Robert and this is my wife, Tina."

"Nice to meet you. Do you guys want to sit?" I ask.

"Oh, sure. Let me buy you guys a drink," he says, looking around for the waiter. Tina's face looks embarrassed by her husband but also like she's used to it.

"Honey, they don't want to be bothered by an old couple like us."

"We don't mind," I say, looking over at Cruz.

"We could use a drink," Cruz says.

I get up from my seat and walk over to sit next to Cruz. Robert and Tina scoot themselves into the booth. The waiter comes around and Robert orders us a pitcher of their house beer.

"So are you guys here for business or pleasure?" Robert asks.

"Both. I came to pick up some wine for my brewery and we made a weekend getaway out of it," Cruz explains.

"We'll have to come by sometimes and see it," Tina says.

"Yes, do. I would love to have you two," Cruz says.

The waiter drops off our beers and we all clink our cups together and take a sip. The atmosphere around here is relaxing. People look like they come here to grab a bite to eat and chill with their friends. I'm wondering why Cruz doesn't know more people here if he comes here often to pick up wine.

"How long have you two love birds been together?" Robert asks.

We both stay silent. Neither one of us knows what to say.

"Honey, stop being nosey," Tina says and drops her head into her hands in embarrassment.

"It's okay. We're not together," Cruz says.

Both of their faces drop in confusion. "Man, she's beautiful. You better snatch her up before someone else does." Robert gives me a wink.

Both of my cheeks heat with a smile. A chuckle comes out of

Cruz as he rests his hand on my thigh. A chill runs up my body, giving me goose bumps.

"We're trying to see how things go," he says and looks over at me.

A bashful smile comes out of me.

We ended up staying in the brewery for the rest of the night. Robert and Tina ordered another pitcher of beer. Despite the fact that Cruz and I were taking our time, they made sure they finished the pitchers. I'm taken aback by how much they can drink. But I suppose with age they have a higher tolerance.

Cruz looks over to see if I'm ready to leave. I nod in agreement and return my attention to Robert and Tina. "Well, I think we're going to head out. We're pretty beat. It was nice to meet you guys."

"Okay. We better get going too, honey," Tina says to her husband.

We all scoot ourselves off the booth. Robert and Tina both lean in and give me a hug. "Thanks for letting us join you," Robert says.

"I had a lot of fun." I step aside as Tina gives Cruz a hug and Robert reaches out to shake Cruz's hand.

"You better not let this one get away," Robert says and points toward me.

Cruz gazes at me with a smile. "I won't," he says with a wink.

After saying our goodbyes, we both stumble our way back to our hotel. Once inside our room, Cruz heads straight for the bed, laying his back down on the mattress, with his feet still on the floor.

"I'm going to take a quick shower," I say.

Cruz nods. I head over to the bathroom to wash off the day's sweat from riding our bikes all day.

Once I'm done, I head back out and see Cruz still in the same spot. I tiptoe over to the bed to slide in, not wanting to wake him up. But right away, he looks over at me and asks, "How was your shower?"

"Oh, did I wake you up?" I whisper as I slide under the covers.

"No. I wasn't asleep."

"It feels good to be clean after being in the sun all day," I say.

Cruz gets up off the bed and walks over to this duffle bag and pulls out what looks like boxer briefs. "My turn."

I'm dozing off to sleep when I hear the bathroom door open up. My eyes go wide at the sight of Cruz. He comes out with only boxer briefs on accentuating the bulge he has down there. I sink a little deeper into the mattress so he doesn't see me eyeing him. His back is toward me while he places something in his duffle bag. I can't help but notice his broad back and muscular arms. His body appears to be built like he didn't have to work day in and day out at the gym. He walks over to the bed and gets under the covers with me. His body heat radiates toward me, making my center heat and ache with the sight of him.

Cruz turns his body over toward me. "Did you have fun tonight?"

"Yes, I did. Did you?"

"Yes. It was nice to get away with someone for once," he says with a yawn.

"Do you not get away much?"

He shrugs his shoulders. "Not very often, and if I do, it's by myself. With starting the brewery and building my home, I haven't had a lot of time."

"That must have been a lot of work doing both around the same time." I turn around onto my side and face him. "Thanks for the dance and for taking me here. It was a nice little getaway."

"Anytime. I hope it helped clear your mind a bit."

"What makes you think I needed to clear my mind?" Is he referring to that night at his house when I got too emotional?

"I figured with you traveling over here, it would be nice to slow things down and relax."

Cruz's thoughtfulness surprises me. I've never been in a relationship with someone like that before. He took me with him, I assume, because of my reaction at his house. But he's too respectful to bring that night up again.

I give him a small smile and watch as another yawn escapes him. Sleep quickly absorbs both of us.

CHAPTER FOURTEEN

Tessa

AC HITS me like a brick of ice, causing a shiver to run through me as I walk into the brewery. That is one thing I hate about the summer. You turn into an icicle when you enter an air-conditioned building after being outside in the heat. But I'd prefer to deal with that than the winter cold.

Thoughts of Cruz are making me feel happy after our weekend together. It's been a while since I've felt this good. I was counting down the minutes until the end of my shift so I could go to the brewery and see him.

"Hey," I say.

"Hi," Ashley says in a shrieky voice and wraps me up in her arms. "How was your weekend?" She waggles her eyebrows up and down repeatedly.

"It was fun."

"You're just like Cruz. You both answer with little to no words." She rolls her eyes. "How about I come over after work and we have drinks and you can tell me all about it?"

"Deal."

"Are you staying or did you stop by to say hi?"

"I came to say hi and have a drink."

The door behind me opens up and more people are coming in for the dinner rush hour. "Go ahead and seat them. I'm going to run to the bathroom," I say.

Once I'm done in the bathroom, I head back out to the hostess stand. More people have come in, so I wait on the side for Ashley to finish seating them. A big party follows her back and I look around, searching for Cruz. Sometimes he's at the bar, but I don't see him. He must be in the back. Ashley catches my attention when she heads back over toward me.

"Bar or table?" she asks.

Before I can answer, the door is swinging open again. I glance over at the guy walking in and my whole body stiffens. The blood drains from my face. The noises around me sound like static coming from a TV. It feels as if the world has stopped moving and it's only me and him in this separate dimension. His eyes are wide and his mouth has dropped. My legs feel like rubber, making it hard for me to take the next step.

Ashley grabs my shoulder and wiggles me out of the stiffness. I jump back and look at her. Her eyes are squinting in confusion at my actions. "Hey. Are you okay?"

I remain silent. All my questions swarm my thoughts. What the fuck is he doing here? Did he follow me? Has he known I've been here this whole time? I take a few steps sideways as I watch him glare at me. As I try to hurry out the door, I run into a hardened chest and masculine hands come up and grab my arms, catching me from a fall. I throw my arms out of the hold and look up and see Cruz wide-eyed.

"What's wrong?" he says.

I look back at Chris and run. Once I'm outside, I round the corner and head down the alleyway to the back of the brewery. I stop and rest my back on the wall, out of sight, listening to hear if Chris has followed me. But the only person I hear is Cruz calling my name. Once I hear nothing, I run back to my place.

I'm wandering around in circles in my studio, wondering how and why Chris is here. He doesn't like to travel. Because of that, I left thinking he wouldn't follow me, so why is he here? Did he come here alone? But the shock on his face seeing me only tells me he must not have known I was here, either. I open the fridge and pop open a beer to help calm my nerves. He didn't follow me out. Maybe he doesn't care for me or us anymore.

The sun has set and I've been waiting for any kind of noise. None have come until I hear footsteps coming up the stairs outside. I hurry and switch off my light and stand still by the door. Making sure I make no sounds.

"Tessa," Ashley says with a small knock on the door.

I'm waiting for her to leave as I stand here in silence. She's going to ask me what happened and I don't know what to say because I don't even know what happened.

Another knock comes through. "Tessa, open up. I know you're in there. Cruz and I are worried about you. We've been calling and texting you and you don't answer."

I've left my phone on vibrate so I could hear any little sound that comes my way and I haven't looked at it since. Ashley knocks a few more times and then I hear her footsteps walking down the stairs. I grab my phone and lie on the bed. There are multiple text messages and missed calls from both Ashley and Cruz. A tear runs down my face. As much as I try to stop them, they keep flowing out of me.

It's safe to say I didn't sleep at all last night. I realized I wasn't going to get any sleep once the sun came up. Forcing myself out of bed, I walk over to the bathroom and see my bloodshot, puffy eyes staring back at me in the mirror. Cold water doesn't even help the puffiness.

The shop doesn't open for a few hours. Last night I decided to lie low here for a few days. Hoping Chris was only here to visit and leave. I'm not one to hide, but I don't have the energy to run into him again. Sometimes you need to be *done*, not mad, not upset, just *done*. I've been through this enough times with my mom to know that you have to walk away. The answers to the questions I have for that night I know will not be the truth, especially if he is still using. There is no use wasting my time. I didn't pack up and leave my life to run into him again. When I left, I left for good. Leaving everything from my past behind.

I turn on music and jump into the shower to get my mind off things and start this day fresh. I called June and let her know I came down with something and would need the day off. She didn't sound too upset. I hope she doesn't think this is a constant thing about me taking off. Cruz and I only got back from Palisade a few days ago.

I'm sitting here, enjoying the pancakes I made, and a knock comes through my door.

"Tessa!" Ashley yells. I'm taken aback at how abruptly she said my name.

I texted Ashley and Cruz back, letting them know I came down with something that I slept through the whole evening and night. There is no need to get anyone worried about this. Chris will be gone soon.

I get up and walk over to my door and open it enough for her to see my face. She looks at me with a dead stare.

"Hey. Did you receive my text?" That's all I can think to say.

"Oh, the one where you were supposedly sick. You had us worried all night. And that's all the explanation we get from you.

I know we don't know each other that well. I thought we had a pretty good relationship so far that you didn't need to lie to me."

Her words catch me off guard. I step away from the door and turn my back to her. She places her hand on my back, trying to comfort me. This is something I've never had with a friend before. She walks me over to the table and we both sit facing each other.

"What happened? What's going on?" she mumbles. We both take a seat at my small two-seat kitchen table I bought from the shop.

"I don't want this to be a big deal. That's why I left and stayed home the rest of the night."

"What's going on? Why would this be a big deal? Who was that guy who walked into the brewery last night?"

All the questions she's bombarded me with are causing me to shake. "Will you please trust me on this and know I'm okay?"

She nods and says nothing. I know deep down she knows what's going on, but she said before she doesn't pry into people's lives. "You should come up with something better to say to Cruz, though."

I sit up and pull back slightly. "Why?"

"He stayed up all night parked outside to make sure that guy didn't come to your place."

"What!"

She nods back to me.

"This is what I mean. I didn't want to make such a big deal out of this."

"It's kind of hard to not make such a big deal with how abruptly you left the brewery. And you never responded to our messages last night. Only for us to receive a text the next morning saying that you were sick. I'm thinking you're not one to let anyone in easily. I actually like our friendship and I'm going to be worried. I also will not let Cruz get hurt over someone, so if this is all a game to you, leave him out of it. He doesn't deserve this."

Flutters form in the pit of my stomach. My breathing has become shallow, trying to find the right words to say. I grew up thinking no one wanted to deal with someone's trauma. My grandparents are the only ones who cared. Not even my best friend Mila knew how to talk to me when I was dealing with moments of sadness that would overwhelm me. I learned to keep it to myself and not drag anyone else down with me. Tears blur my eyes and roll down my cheeks.

"I'm not used to anyone caring this much. This is new to me." My voice shakes. "I never meant to worry you guys. I don't want to be a burden."

"You're not a burden if we like you," she says with a chuckle.

I clear my throat. "That guy was the reason I ran away," I say with finger quotation marks. "I never thought he would find me because he doesn't even like to travel. Out of all the places I run to, I find the most well-known place of all." I shrug my shoulders. "Just my luck, I guess."

She sits in front of me, waiting for me to go on. I let out an enormous sigh. "I woke up one night on the floor, hazy from a physical fight we had. That was the first time he laid his hands on me and the last. I picked up and left. So everyone here was right. I ran away. I don't know what he is doing here, but the surprise on his face makes me think he didn't expect to see me either." I sit up taller in my chair and wipe the tears from my face. "All I wanted was a fresh start. I grew up watching my mom do drugs and her lowlife boyfriends beating her. I never thought I would go through that. Chris came home one night drugged out, and I knew what was going to happen next. The life I left behind is full of trauma. Even after finding out this place was popular, I only stayed because of you and Cruz."

"You know those situations are more common than you think."

My face rises in question. "What do you mean?" The older I get, the more I'm finding out how common this is. It's the sad truth. And how common it is for people to keep it hushed.

"I left my family to come back here to get away from an abusive boyfriend. He was physically and mentally abusive, and I stayed way too many times to count. Until I spiraled out into a deep hole that I didn't know how to get myself out of. My life was a total lie. No one knew what I was going through. I guess I hid it well. My ex and I knew how to keep up our appearances to make it seem like we were a happy couple. But deep down inside, I was hurting. One day, I picked up and left just like you. He never cared that I left. I think he was waiting for me to be done because I never received one phone call from him asking where I went. Right then I knew nothing would have changed, and I made the right decision."

My heart sinks, knowing someone as genuine as Ashley went through that. "Do your parents know why you left?"

"To my knowledge, no. But you never know what people really know. Just like you, I didn't want to get them involved, so I understand where you are coming from."

I let out a long breath that I didn't even know I was holding in. "Does Cruz know about your ex?"

"Yes, he knows."

"I don't want Cruz to think I'm some trauma case. And..." I'm having a hard time saying it aloud. I'm not in the right position mentally to start something new. Sometimes I can't help what I feel. He's been so gentle and patient with me it's hard not to fall fast for someone like that.

"And what?"

"I think... I'm falling for Cruz and I don't think that's the best thing to do right now."

She raises her eyebrows as if it's dumb of me to think that.

"He's falling for you, too. I can see it. And he wouldn't have sat outside all night, making sure you were okay, if he thought you were a trauma case."

"Could we keep this between us two? I'll talk to Cruz about it when I'm ready. Just not right now."

Ashley stands up from the chair and says, "Fine by me. I'll stay out of it. I have to get going, though."

I stand up and give her a hug. "Thanks for stopping by."

"Call me if you need anything," she says, heading out the door.

"I will." I shut the door, then lie back down to try to fall asleep.

CHAPTER FIFTEEN

Tessa

BEFORE MY DAY starts at the Antique Shop, I want to run out and get some coffee. Since my first day here, I haven't been back to the Corner Café. I haven't seen Cheri either. I've been meaning to stop by and tell her thanks for pointing me to the Antique Shop. Because of her, I landed a job and a place to stay all on the same day.

After staying inside for a few days, it feels good to get some fresh air. Cruz hasn't pushed to know what happened. I'm assuming Ashely had something to do with that. I trust she didn't tell him everything. Hopefully, she didn't. But that might be my problem. I trust too easily. Maybe she didn't even have an abusive boyfriend, and she was trying to make me feel better. It worked. I shake those thoughts out of my head and keep heading toward the café. Ashley is a good person. She wouldn't do that.

When someone breaks your trust, it's crazy how much you can overthink. Especially when it's from a parent. I remember my mom always saying, *This will be the last time. No more boyfriends. He's a good guy. Nothing happened.* I had to stop asking my mom questions, knowing the same words and actions would repeat.

The bell at the top of the café's door rings as I walk in. Right away, I hear my name. Cheri comes my way with a notepad in her hand.

"Hey, Tessa! I haven't seen you around. I thought you decided not to stay."

"Hey! Yup, I'm here. I stayed thanks to you. I got a job and a place to stay all on the same day."

"Oh good. So you got a job at the Antique Shop?"

"Yeah. And June has a studio on top of the shop that she rented out to me."

"Nice. I'm happy everything worked out. I need to get back to work. Today is a busy day and I'm not even sure why. Don't be a stranger." She walks away to serve a table.

"I won't. See you around."

The second I step outside with an iced coffee in my hand, the heat blazes down on my skin as if I'm two feet away from the sun. Every day, it seems like it's getting hotter.

I bend my head down a little as I insert the shop's key into the front door to open up for the day. Once the door is unlocked, I raise my head and notice a shadow reflecting off the window. I turn my head to where the shadow is standing and jump in surprise. It's Cruz coming my way. I lift my arm to my forehead, trying to cover the sun shining toward my eyes to get a better look.

"Hey." I smile at Cruz. I open the door a little wider and step in to get us both out of the heat.

"Hi," he says.

I walk over to the desk that holds the cash register, set my coffee down, and turn back to Cruz. He seems a little on edge right now or mad. I can't read him very well.

"Is everything okay?" I question.

"I should ask you the same thing."

Silence fills the air as I struggle to find the right words. Cruz and I haven't spoken yet. To be honest, I wasn't sure what to say after Ashley told me he stayed outside all night to make sure Chris didn't come by. Although right now, I'm not sure if he knows who Chris is. Ashley said she would stay out of it.

"I'm doing well," I say hesitantly. I reach over, grab my coffee, and take a sip. "If I had known you were coming by, I would have got you a coffee." I shake the ice around in my cup.

Cruz squints his eyebrows at me with a dead stare. "Are you going to ignore the other day?"

My shoulders slump down and I shake my head a little. "I really want to keep this to myself until I'm ready to talk about it."

"You don't like to open up to people, do you?"

I shake my head. "I left a life behind that I would like to keep behind me."

"But it doesn't seem like that life left you." Cruz walks a little closer to me and places his hand on mine. "I'm a private person too, so I'll respect that. Just know that we're here for you."

"Who's we?"

"Me and Ashley. Who else?"

"Oh, right. Of course. I know." The creaks of the door pull me out of my daze of wondering what to say next to Cruz. "I better get to work," I say with a smile.

"Okay. Promise me you'll call me if you need anything?"

"I promise."

Cruz comes closer to me and kisses me on my forehead. I gaze at him, smile, and then watch him turn toward the exit.

I make my way to the customers who just walked in. "Hi, is there anything I can help you look for?"

The middle-aged couple look at me and say, "Just looking."

"If you have questions, I'll be over here." I point to the desk. Both nod their heads.

Saved by the bell. I wasn't sure how far Cruz would push. If it wasn't for customers walking in, he might have asked more questions.

I hear June come in from the back and turn around to greet her. "Hi, June."

She walks closer to me and sets her coffee cup on the counter. "Are you feeling better?"

"Yes. A lot better. Thank you for letting me take a few days off at the last minute."

"Well, what else was I supposed to do? Make you come in and get me and the customers sick?" she says in a sarcastic tone.

June is a very blunt person. Does she know she can come off as rude? I have a strong sense she knows and doesn't care.

"No, I guess not."

"By the way, some guy came looking for you the other day."

"What! What guy?"

June walks away to the back, not answering my question.

I follow her back and ask again, "June, what guy?"

"Look, I'm not one to get into someone's business. But when some random girl shows up here asking for a job and then some random guy shows up looking for that person. It looks suspicious, okay. I don't want to be in the middle of it. I'm too old to be in the middle of it."

"June! What did he look like?"

She turns and faces me. "Average height, brown army cut hair. He wore a wife beater and some shorts."

This cannot be happening.

"Don't worry. I didn't tell him I knew you."

"Oh," I say, shocked. "What did he say?"

June grabs a box cutter and starts opening the shipment we got this week. I walk over to the box and start pulling the items out and unwrap the bubble wrap.

"He said he was looking for a friend and described you. I said I don't know anyone who looks like that." She hands me a lamp. "Now get back to work and start finding places to put these out on the floor."

I take the lamp from her and walk away to the floor. Chris being here for a few days is making a bigger scene than I thought it would. This wasn't the man I used to know. Moving in together, you would think I knew him enough. He did a one-eighty overnight. I keep replaying the last year of my life with him. Wondering when or what would have made him flip a switch. Did I miss something? I hope this is the end of seeing him again, but my gut tells me it's not.

CHAPTER SIXTEEN

Tessa

"ASHLEY!" I yell before the water swallows me whole. I kick myself off the pool's ground and swim back up to the surface. "You better get your ass in here now," I say while wiping my eyes free of chlorine water.

Ashley erupts in laughter after pushing me in. Then I watch as her eyes widen and her arms go up in the air, trying to catch her balance. Cruz quietly walked up behind her and pushed her in. A big splash comes from the pool once she hits the water. She swims back up, throwing her long hair back and wiping her eyes.

"What the hell?" she yells.

I shrug and look behind her.

She turns around and sees Cruz convulsing with laughter. "Oh, you think you're so funny?"

Cruz says nothing as he walks back over to the grill with both of his shoulders vibrating with laughter.

Both of us swim over to the edge and lean our arms on the

cement and let our legs float in the water. This past month has been in the triple digits. The heat is so dry here it's sometimes hard to catch a breath. The sun heats Cruz's pool to where sometimes it feels like a hot tub.

"You know what? You've loosened him up," Ashley says.

I watch Cruz grill our burgers. He wanted to have another BBQ since it's the Fourth of July weekend. The same people he had over last time came swimming again. Jason, Caleb, and Marnie. All three men huddle around the grill talking and Marnie heads into the pool to join us with three Coronas in her hand.

"Hey, Marnie, how are you?" Ashley asks.

Marnie hands us each a beer. "Good. How are you guys? Haven't seen you since the last time we were here. I'm shocked Cruz had another get-together so soon after."

I grab the Corona and take a sip. "Ashley was telling me he's loosened up."

"No. I said you've loosened him up," she says.

"I can see that," Marnie says while she looks over at the guys talking.

"I don't know what I did," I say.

Marnie turns back over to us and says, "I think you make him happier."

"She does make him happier," Ashley agrees with Marnie.

I look over at Cruz and watch him laughing and bullshitting with the guys. His face looks a lot brighter since I've met him. I never realized before. I feel lighter too after meeting him. Like no matter what happens, he'll be there for me. I've never had that. Except for my grandparents. But the love between grandchildren and grandparents differs from the love you have from a partner or your own parents.

"Are you guys together now?" Marnie asks.

"No. We barely started hanging out. We haven't gotten to that point to talk about that."

"Oh, come on. You guys are going to end up together, anyway. What is there to talk about?" Ashley says.

"If this is something we want to move forward with."

Both Marnie and Ashley look at me and start giggling.

"What?" I say.

"Obviously, it is something you both want if you guys keep hanging out," Ashley mutters and rolls her eyes at me. "Not to mention how both of your faces light up when around one another."

"Well…we need more time." I clench my jaw together and face Ashley to get her to shut up. She acts like we haven't talked about how I was feeling toward Cruz the other day and how nervous I've been about starting something new so soon.

She must understand my expression because she stops talking about it.

I hear a bit of commotion behind us and see an older lady step onto the porch and reach in for a hug from Cruz.

"Time to meet the mother," Ashley says.

"What!" I exclaim. Saying that a little too loud, everyone looks over at me. I give a little wave and my head gets a little woozy.

"Don't worry. She's very chill. You'll like her," Ashley says as I follow Marnie and Ashley out of the pool.

You never get over the nervousness of meeting the parents. I step out of the pool, stumbling on my own feet, and Cruz catches me before I slip and fall.

"Are you okay?" he asks.

"Yes. Why didn't you tell me your mom was coming over?" I whisper.

"I didn't know she was. It will be fine," he mumbles. He takes hold of my hand and leads me to his mother.

"Mom, this is Tessa. Tessa, this is my mom, Janet."

"Tessa! It's so nice to meet you. I've heard great things about you." She wraps me in a small hug, like she's trying not to get wet.

"Oh," I say, stunned. "Well, I hope they are all good things."

"Oh yes, they are," she says with her eyebrows raised. "I wanted to drop off some stuff I got at a local market for you," she says to Cruz while handing him a bag.

"Thanks, Mom. Do you want to stay and have a burger? They're almost done."

"No, honey. I'm meeting Suzy for dinner or else I would," she says with a charming smile on her face.

Janet hugs us all again while saying her goodbyes. I'm a little relieved. I didn't expect to meet any parents today. Especially Cruz's.

The sun has finally gone down and we're out front, sitting on the lawn with blankets underneath us. Jason and Caleb both bought fireworks they wanted to light tonight.

Cruz joins me from behind, puts his legs around me, and falls back on his hands. When I turn back, I see him smile at me, and my cheeks flush. I uncross my legs and lean my back against his chest. He reaches down and kisses me on the cheek.

We all watch Jason and Caleb light the fireworks and all the colors come to life. We're all a little drunk, cheering the guys every time a firework lights up. Marnie more than us. She's cheering Caleb on every time he lights one up, as if this is a competition. Such a supportive girlfriend, even when all he's doing is lighting up fireworks.

I lean my head back and look up at Cruz, watching them light the fireworks. He looks down at me and inches his way closer to my lips. I turn my body a little to the left and shift my head closer to him. The heat of his breath comes closer until we lock our lips together. He pulls my body in closer to him and kisses me gently. I reach my arm around his head and bring him closer to my lips.

"Get a room!" Ashley yells.

While our lips are still locked together, we both open our eyes, look at each other, and smile. We release each other and I turn back around. As I scoot closer to him, getting in a comfortable position, I feel a hard bulge between us.

"Look what you do to me," he says, rubbing himself on me.

"We'll have to do something about that then," I mutter.

"Why wait?"

"Um, because you have people over."

"I guess you're right." He sighs.

I yelp from the spanking Cruz gives my ass. "Stop it, people are going to see you."

"So?"

We're all cleaning up the aftermath of tonight. Everyone is bringing stuff to the kitchen from outside while Cruz and I put it away. Giving Cruz more chances to slap my ass since we're the only two in here. After putting some condiments away in the fridge, I turn around and crash into Cruz's chest. He reaches down and grabs my ass, pulling me closer to him, and pulls my lips into his mouth and sucks on my bottom lip. His grip is so close to my center I'm aching for his hand to come around and touch me.

"I think that's our cue to leave," Caleb says.

"I think it is too," Cruz says. I look over at all of them standing in the doorway of the back patio, watching and giggling.

Cruz releases me from his hold and turns around and says, "Thanks for helping clean up."

"No problem, man," Jason says and pats Cruz on the back.

"You're probably going to have more to clean up tonight." He gives us a wink.

I reach out and give Marnie a hug while Caleb holds her up.

"You better get this man laid," she says. "I'm going to do the same with this one right here." She pats Caleb's chest with her eyes half open.

Caleb rolls his eyes and says bye to me. "Yeah, I would love to see how that goes, babe," he says to Marnie and we all laugh.

We all say our goodbyes and Ashley whispers into my ear, "Get it, girl."

"Shut up," I say.

Cruz and I follow them out the front door, watching them get into their cars and drive away. I step back and gaze at him as he closes the front door. His stare shows he is about to tackle me. I turn away from him and squeal my way into the kitchen. He corners me into the kitchen and reaches out to pick me up, and I wrap my legs around his waist as he places me on the kitchen island. He takes my face and kisses me as if I've never been kissed before. His touch causes a reaction in my body. My legs tighten around him, drawing him in. He's between my legs, and I can feel his bulge pounding against my midsection. He stops kissing me, releases my face, and places me on my back.

I look around and see beer and liquor bottles everyone carried in from outside all around me. He drags his tongue down my neck, softly kissing me. When he goes for my chest, my back arches to allow him to kiss me more deeply. He reaches behind my back and snaps the top of my swimsuit off, releasing my breasts. He places one hand on my breast and squeezes it while sucking on my other nipple. His lips travel down to my core and then to my left thigh while he sucks my inner leg, making me want him even more. I shift my weight closer to his mouth.

"Eager, are we?" he says.

My hands curl around his hair, drawing him closer. His tongue moves closer to my center, taunting me. My breathing becomes labored as I anticipate what is to follow. Then he wraps his tongue over my clit, making me pant even more. My clit is pulsing from the movements of his tongue. My entire body tenses, and my back arches even more. Then I feel the relief as my entire body shakes from the orgasm coursing through me.

He picks me up and wraps my legs around his torso, carrying me to his bedroom and placing me on his bed. He strolls over to his nightstand, takes a condom, rips it open, and slides it down his shaft.

As he hovers over me, leans down, and pulls me into a kiss, the bed sinks in. I spread my legs wider to allow him to get in deeper. I release a breath I didn't realize I was holding the moment he penetrates me. Slowly, he thrusts, stretching me to his size. He quickens his speed, moving in a rhythm that feels amazing, and my moans get louder and his breathing deepens. He quickens his pace, leans into my neck, and convulses on top of me.

CHAPTER SEVENTEEN

MY THROBBING HEAD wakes me up from the aftermath of drinking last night, making it hard for me to fall back asleep. I tossed and turned for what felt like hours before I finally gave up on sleeping. Cruz's chest rises and falls as he breathes deeply in his sleep. Trying not to wake him up, I slide out of his bed and head for the bathroom outside of his master bedroom. I don't want to wake him while I take a shower to see if that helps with my headache. As the shower starts, I remember I don't have extra clothes here. I slip back into the room and pick a T-shirt from his closet.

The shower did little for my headache. I'm now standing here, waiting for my coffee to brew as I watch the sunrise from the back patio. I don't remember the last time I've been up this early to watch the sunrise. The smell of the outside summer day helps release the tension from my hangover as I sit and watch the sky light up in different colors. I bring the coffee mug to my lips and inhale the scent. My lips rise from the small smile that forms. I can't remember when I've been this happy or content with my life. My life hasn't always been about what I want. I've never been content with where I was at. Living back home, I always worried when my mother was going to come back and ruin the life I built with my grandparents. I felt a little at ease when I met Chris because I trusted him with my past and told him everything. But the feeling I had with him never felt like this. I thought I was safe with him, but now I know I never was. Maybe I learned some sort of security from him. I never realized what it really should feel like until now. I push my thoughts out of my head, trying not to overthink and enjoy this moment.

Opening the pantry to the kitchen to see what breakfast Cruz has, I pull a pancake mix out and get to making them.

As I'm about done making the pancakes, arms wrap around me and warm lips kiss me on my neck.

"You didn't have to make breakfast."

"I couldn't sleep. So I sat up and watched the sunrise and then made pancakes. Serve yourself some before they get cold."

Cruz grabs one off the plate I have them stacked on and shoves half of it in his mouth.

"That's how you're going to eat them?" I ask.

"Only this one. I'll wait for you to be done so we can eat them together."

He walks over to the coffee and brews himself a cup. "Do you want one?"

"Sure. Thanks."

We're both sitting at the table, buttering our pancakes and pouring syrup on them. "I could get used to this," he says.

"What? Having a housewife?"

"No, going to bed with you, waking up to you, and sitting down to eat our meals together. Not to mention waking up and finding you in my T-shirt." He raises his eyebrows up and down. "It's sexy."

I snicker. "I didn't know my lack of clothes would turn you on."

"It's not the lack of clothes, it's you in my clothes that's sexy. The lack of clothes is a plus. Help yourself to my closet anytime."

I reach over and pour myself some milk, trying to help wash away the sweetness of the pancakes. "So you've never done this before?"

"Done what?"

"Lived with a girl?" I say as I move my eyes around to our surroundings.

He shakes his head. "Have you lived with a guy?"

"Once. For a little while."

He stays silent, chewing his pancake.

"Does that bug you?"

"No. I guess I'm more jealous."

"Jealous! Jealous of what?"

"Someone else having this with you before me."

"Aww, that's cute." I watch Cruz's cheeks go a shade of light pink. I run my hand over his cheek and say, "There is nothing to be jealous about. This right here is more than I ever had living with that other person."

"Good!"

A yawn comes out of me and I lie back against the chair.

"Do you want to go back to bed?"

"Yes. I tried so hard to fall back asleep when I woke up because I knew this would happen. I didn't want to waste my day sleeping."

"I don't find it a waste if you're here with me in my house."

I chuckle. "Don't you have to go to the brewery?"

"No. They should be fine without me. I have to trust them someday. No one has called in and I'm caught up on everything. It should be fine. You don't have to work at the shop today?"

"No. June closed today." I reach out for another pancake and start nibbling at it. These casual conversions with Cruz make me feel closer to him. Sometimes I want them to go all day and night. But then he'll probably think I'm crazy.

"How do you like working with June?" He takes a drink of his coffee.

"I thought it would be hard at first because of how blunt she is. Sometimes it can come off as rude. But once I got to know her and I'm around her more, I assume she's not trying to be rude and that's just her personality. Or so I hope."

Cruz chuckles. "Yeah, she can be very blunt."

"Has she ever been married? She doesn't open up that much. Well, I guess I don't either." I shrug.

"Not that I know of."

A yawn comes through me again, and Cruz stands up and reaches for my hand. "Let's go back to bed." I take his hand and follow him back to his room. The second my head hits the pillow, sleep takes over me.

CHAPTER EIGHTEEN

Tessa

THE FOLLOWING DAY, Cruz rushed to an emergency at the brewery. He dropped me back off at my place. After waking up from our nap, we spent all day in bed watching movies, talking, and eating. Being present with him was a nice change of pace. We both have never done that before. It was different because usually I'm up doing something and so is he.

I'm still so relaxed from yesterday as I struggle to walk up the stairs. I'm not in the mood to do anything again today. But I have to work today. As I enter my studio, I'm wrapped up in someone's arms. The familiar, uneasy hug I receive catches me off guard. I extend both arms toward his chest and forcefully push him away. My eyes follow him as he tumbles backward.

"What the fuck are you doing here?" I yell.

He covers his mouth with his hands, looking at me wide-eyed. "I can't believe what I'm seeing. It's you. It's really you."

"What the hell are talking about, you fucking idiot?" I say

with heavy breaths, trying to calm the anger that's boiling up inside me.

"I thought." He runs his hands through his hair.

"You thought what?"

"That night. I thought..." He paces back and forth.

I stand there, watching his beaded sweat drip from his hair-line. He paces back and forth, agitated about something. He's either coming down from something or is still on it. I can't deal with this today. I never wanted to deal with this again. To get him to stop pacing, I walk up to him and push on his shoulder. He looks at me, forgetting I'm there. My room. My studio. He brings his hand up toward my face and I slap it away.

"What the fuck do you want, Chris?" I yell as I concentrate on his dilated pupils.

"I thought. I thought I hurt you," he says with his eyes wide.

"You did hurt me. Why do you think I left?"

He wobbles his head. "No! I mean, I thought I hurt you for good."

"What! You thought you killed me?"

He looks at me wide-eyed and nods.

"Well, lucky for you, you didn't. And how nice of you to think you killed me and you did nothing about it."

"I'm so sorry."

"For what? Do you even know what you did?"

He paces around the room again. "I woke up at a friend's house and had this recollection of me choking you. I hurried home to see if you were okay, but you were already gone. So was all your stuff. I couldn't remember anything else and I couldn't stop replaying that night in my head. I thought I did something worse and buried you somewhere. I searched everywhere I could have buried you but found nothing. I didn't want to go to your grandparents because what if I really did something and they got spooked and called the police on me?"

His mouth is running a hundred miles a minute. It sounds

like it took everything in him to say that. Once he's done, he's trying to catch his breath.

"That's nice to know you are worried about yourself more than me. You're an idiot."

"What! Don't you see I've been worried this whole time and freaking out," he says with his arms down by his sides and his hands in fists. "I haven't slept or eaten in months. And now I'm being haunted by something. I see shadows all around me. Everywhere I go. They follow me everywhere. I can't get rid of them."

"I don't know what drugs you are on. There is something wrong with you. After hearing your pathetic speech, it only shows me you weren't worried that much."

"I'm not on drugs," he says with a side-eye, as if he's trying to hide his eyes from me.

"Come on. I'm not stupid. You know I would be able to tell. It's pathetic of you to sit here and lie to me and you're being haunted now. What else could it be?"

He gets down on his knees before me. "Please forgive me. I love you. I want you to come back."

"No. We're done. I'm not coming back. So get the fuck out!" I scream.

"Why don't you care?"

"What! Care about what? You?"

He nods his head.

"I gave all my trust to you and told you about my past. I don't usually open up, but I did with you. And you turned out to be exactly what I grew up with. So no, I do not care about you anymore. I don't even know what happened that night. You did a one-eighty overnight. You're not the person I once knew. I don't want you. I don't want to deal with you or this bullshit."

"We can start over." He stands up in front of me.

"Oh right, because I want to be in a relationship where I have to sleep with one eye open and wonder if you're going to come home sober or not. Have you been on drugs this whole time and I was too dumb to see it?"

"What! I'm not on drugs."

"Get out!" I yell and push him toward the door. "I came here to start a new life. You're not ruining this for me."

His eyes open wide in shock and he allows me to push him out the door. I slam the door shut and lock it. I run over to the window above the kitchen sink and watch him walk away. My hands run through my hair as I let out a heavy sigh. I walk over to the door and inspect if it's broken, but it's not. He broke in here somehow and I don't know how. I'm going to have to change the locks. If that even helps. Or consider a different locking system.

I rush over to the bathroom and throw my hair up into a bun and swipe a few strokes of mascara onto my eyelashes. I'm already late for work. I strip out of my clothes, put on a fresh pair of underwear, a T-shirt, shorts, and slip my sandals on as I stumble down to the back of the shop.

June is showing people around the store when I arrive at the counter. There is a box open on top of it half full. I unwrap the remaining items in the box to distract myself and stay occupied with work. I pray Chris doesn't come in here and make a scene. His behavior is so erratic, I don't know what to expect from him. He never acted like this when we were together. He's a whole different person. I don't even know him.

June walks over to me, and I smile at her. "Hi, June. Sorry I'm late."

She stops and stares at me with a stern look on her face. "Is everything okay?"

"Yes," I say reluctantly.

She shakes her head and walks to the other side of the counter. "My ears may be old, but I heard screaming up there. Is this going to be a problem?"

"No," I mumble.

June gives me another stern look and walks away from me.

Relief washed over me as I closed up and turned off the open sign.

I jumped and got goose bumps every time the door creaked. I was lucky tonight, but how long will it last? The sound of my phone ringing frightens me. *Calm down.*

"Hello."

"I felt like I haven't heard your beautiful voice in ages," Cruz says on the line.

My shoulders slump down and the tension I've been holding in all day disappears at the sound of Cruz's voice. "I miss you," I say in an unhappy tone.

"Is everything okay? You sound sad."

"It's been a long day."

"Walk over to the window in front of the shop," he says.

Steadying my steps toward the front, when I reach the window, I see Cruz leaning against his truck with pink and white daisies in his hands. I throw my phone in my back pocket, unlock the door, rush over to him, and wrap my arms around him, burying my head into his chest.

"Baby, what's wrong?"

I shake my head while still in his chest. "Nothing. I'm so happy to see you after such a long day."

His hand comes up to my chin and lifts my head up to him. He's staring at me with a concerned look on his face. He moves his head toward my forehead and gives me a kiss. I close my eyes and savor this moment. "Do you want to come home with me?"

"Yes."

"Let's go." He releases his hold on me, opens the door, and helps me in his truck. I watch as he slides into the driver's seat. "I got these for you." He hands me the flowers.

I reach over, grab them, and inhale the scent. "Thank you. They're beautiful."

"Just like you," he says, reaching for my hand and kissing the top of it.

I lean back into the seat and watch as we drive away to his home.

CHAPTER NINETEEN

Cruz

ASHLEY and I are walking through the grocery store, getting the ingredients we need for cocktails to make at the brewery. The smallest costs always add up to be the most. All my bartenders go heavy-handed on minor ingredients. I've told them to stop. But week after week, we run out before shipment comes and I'm having to run to the store at the last minute to stock up. I'm standing at the lime section, picking out limes, waiting for Ashley to bring me a bag to put them in.

"Here," she says, startling me. "You look deep in thought."

"Do I?"

"How are you and Tessa doing?" she asks with a wide smile on her face. Every time she asks me about Tessa, her eyes go bright, waiting for my answer.

"Good."

"Come on, Cruz. Good is not enough to describe what we all see between you two."

I scrunch my eyebrows together. "What do you mean?"

"You both have this blissfulness when you are around each other. Not to mention you are not so uptight anymore."

"I've never been uptight."

She gives me a side-eye. "You show up to work like you're walking on a cloud. You're more interactive with your customers now instead of locking yourself into your office like you usually do."

We both walk over to the pineapples and I watch her touch around and feel for one. "She makes me happy. I don't know what it is. Our connection grew fast. It's easy with her."

"See, aren't you glad I hooked you guys up?"

"You act like you did all the work." Why do my friends think I need help with dating? I know where my feelings were headed. I've known for a while.

"No. But I gave you both a little push." She sets the pineapple into the basket.

"We need blueberries." I point behind her.

"Blueberries? For what?"

I scratch my head. "I don't know. Jason wants to try this new recipe he came up with."

She turns toward the blueberries. "Whatever." She sets them into the cart.

We're walking aisle by aisle, making sure we have everything before we leave. My biggest pet peeve is to turn a customer away from something they ordered. Because I make sure we always have plenty of food in stock. So when I have to do that, it gets under my skin more than it should, so now I always walk down every aisle. Ashley usually comes with me because she's good at doing inventory and knowing what we have and don't have. It's easier for her to remember since I have a lot more stuff running through my head.

"Cruz." I hear my name being called behind me.

I turn around and see June pushing her cart up toward me. "Hi, June."

"Hi, June. How are you?" Ashley says.

"I'm fine. Look, I know you got a thing going on with Tessa, but could you turn your arguing down a notch when you're at her place? I could hear you and I was worried it would scare the customers away," she says with a dead stare.

"What are you talking about, June?"

"Come on, boy, no need to hide it from me. I understand couples argue from time to time and voices get raised, but if you're going to argue at her place, can you wait until after I close?"

I look over at Ashley and she looks just as confused as I am. "June, I've never argued with her at her place. Are you sure she was arguing?"

"Yes. I may be old, but my hearing is still good." June's face drops as she realizes she might have said something she shouldn't have. "I better run along now. Nice seeing you two." She walks away from us.

The other day was when I surprised her and picked her up. I knew something was wrong. But she kept saying she had a long day. I thought she meant at the shop.

"When did you guys argue?" Ashley asks.

"We didn't. It wasn't me." I stand here, trying to recollect who it could've been. The one guy she ran away from is all I can think of. What is going on with her?

"Who could it have been then?"

"I don't know. She only hangs out with us, right?" I look over at Ashley.

"As far as I know." Ashley starts walking ahead of me.

"Ashley! Who was it?"

"I don't know," she says suspiciously.

I take a few bigger steps to catch up to her. "What's going on?"

Ashley says nothing.

"Is she seeing someone else?"

Ashley hurries and shakes her head. "No, Cruz. Don't even think that."

"What else would I think?"

"Give her time to talk to you."

June threw me for a spin. Tessa hasn't been forthcoming about her past. And I accept that. But what if she's pretending to be someone she's not? With my past, it hasn't been simple to open up to someone. But I did it because she is different. I try to see the best in people. It's not always that simple. I can't judge her for not telling me about her past because I'm not forthcoming about my own. Everyone has secrets they'd rather keep to themselves. I hope I'm not wasting my time.

CHAPTER TWENTY

Tessa

"SO THIS IS WHERE YOU LIVE?" I say as I walk into Ashley's house. It's a cute little beige cottage with one bedroom and one bathroom. As I move farther in, I notice a brick fireplace to my right. A tiny love seat is positioned a few feet away from the fireplace.

"Yup. Home sweet home." She shuts the door behind me.

The kitchen is compact, with only enough space for appliances and a small section to walk around in. Hanging from the wall above the stove holds her pots and pans. The counter's gray stone catches my eye as I sit on a barstool. I notice she has a bottle of prosecco on the table. She opens her fridge and pulls out a peach puree and a peach. "I bought stuff to make peach bellinis," she says.

Ashley wanted to have a girls' night with me and catch up. She says I've been spending too much time with Cruz and we both need some girl time. I agreed with her and came over after work. I don't want to lose out on my friendship with her because I started dating Cruz. Even though they're best friends, she hasn't had many girl best friends and enjoys our friendship.

It's been a few days and I haven't seen or heard from Chris. Thank God. I don't know what that day was all about. I hope he got the hint and is going to leave me alone. It's been hard to keep all of this from Cruz. I really don't want it to come between us. My past has come between others before and I hated it. That's why I was never open about it. People always thought being a drug addict is a gene that is passed down by your parents. So when they would hear my mom was a drug addict, they thought I would become one, and no one wants to deal with that.

I'm sitting on a barstool, watching Ashley make our drinks. She's quieter than usual. Something is off. I can feel it. Or maybe that's me reading into it wrong? I decide to let it go. She hands me my drink, and she takes a sip of hers.

"How has work been?" I ask.

"Way too busy. I can't wait till the tourist season is over." She pulls out cheese and meat from the fridge.

"Do you want me to help you with anything?"

"I got it," she says.

I watch as she prepares a charcuterie board for us. "Have you dated anyone since you left Colorado?" I ask.

"Not really. I've gone on a few dates, but nothing ever sticks." She shrugs her shoulders.

"Are they locals or people visiting?"

"People visiting." She finishes up the plate and puts it between the two of us and starts eating off of it.

"Would you ever date a local?"

She chuckles. "No. Everyone knows everyone here. If I was going to be with a local, I would be with one already."

"What if you meet a tourist and he wants to be with you but won't move here? Would you leave to go with him?" I ask.

"If it felt right, I would."

This conversation feels pushed. It's usually easy talking to Ashley. "Ashley, is something going on? You don't sound like yourself. Especially with your short answers that you usually hate getting from people."

She looks at me and takes a sip of her drink and sets it down. "I don't like being lied to."

"What? What are you talking about?" I exclaim.

"I thought there was nothing going on with you and your ex?"

I raise my eyebrows. "Could you elaborate a little more? I don't know what you're talking about. There is nothing going on with anyone else other than Cruz."

She grabs my glass and starts making me another drink.

"Ashley!"

She stops in her tracks and turns to me. "Cruz and I ran into June at the grocery store and she told him that if you guys are going to argue, to keep it down or argue after hours. But the funny thing was it wasn't Cruz you were arguing with."

I lay my head on my hands, holding up the misery this man has caused me in such a short amount of time. If this was his intention to destroy what I built here, he's making it very easy. This is exactly why I keep my past behind me. I didn't want to tell her about him, but I did and now she's questioning me. Which I knew would happen.

I shake my head in my hands. "It's not what you think. I came home from Cruz's and he was there waiting for me inside. I don't even know how he got in because the door was locked."

It's been a couple of days since I saw Cruz. He kept saying he got held up at the brewery with how busy this season is. Was that an excuse? Why hasn't he said anything to me?

"Why haven't you told Cruz anything if it's nothing?"

"Because of this," I say, lifting my hands up. "I tell you about my past and now you're questioning me. If I had told Cruz about my past, he would have done the same thing. I like him, Ashley, and I don't know if I could handle him questioning me like you're doing to me now. I'm not the bad guy here, Chris is, and I'm the one being second-guessed. I know you're looking out for him because of how close you two are. Out of all the people, I thought at least you would understand, given your history, but I guess not." I sigh and take a gulp from my drink. "I really don't want to tell him and leave my past behind."

"You might lose him if you keep it from him."

"How?" I ask.

"Because he asked me if you were seeing someone else. I told him no, but he has been held up in his office for the past two days. I'm not sure what he's been thinking."

"I'll talk to him." Silence spreads across the room. I pop a piece of cheese into my mouth and wash it down with the bellini. "Can we drop this and have the girls' night we wanted to have?"

She nods her head. "Yes! I wasn't going to bring this up, but it was hard not to. Let's erase this and start this night over." She raises her glass to mine. "I'll be right back."

Her back turns away from me and she heads into her bedroom. I slide off the barstool, grab the bottle of Prosecco, and top my glass off. I know Ashley means well, but I can't help but be a little hurt by her questioning me. I guess that's what happens when your friend is best friends with who you're involved with. It's not like she owes me anything. She has more loyalty toward Cruz than me. Which is the way it should be.

Ashley's creating a ruckus in the living room. I get up and go over to see what she's up to. "What are those?" She sets down a white tube with black buttons on top of them.

"It's a pedicure bowl." She passes by me and heads for the kitchen.

I take a seat on the couch in front of the bowl.

Ashley comes back and pours warm water into them. She presses the power button, and it bubbles up. "Put your feet in. It feels amazing."

I kick my sandals off and set my feet in. Ashley takes a seat in front of my bowl. "What are you doing?"

"Giving you a pedicure."

"Oh, I thought we would give ourselves one?"

She grabs a bag of bath salts and pours some in. "I don't mind giving you one. I used to do this back in Colorado."

"Why don't you do them down here?"

She reaches in and pulls one of my feet out and removes my nail polish.

"Cruz needed me at the time and I ended up liking the brewery, so I stayed."

"Well, this is great. I have my own personal pedicurist." I lean back onto the couch as she works on my feet.

The rest of the night lightens up a lot. We had more cocktails, which helped us relax after our earlier conversation. It was nice to have a girls' night out. I haven't had one in a long time. I had lost track of my friends from home. Not that I had many, but we drifted away over time. Finally, having another friend is nice. Especially in a new town.

CHAPTER TWENTY-ONE

I'M WALKING up the stairs to my place and notice a white gift bag sitting by the door. I type in the code to my new door lock a locksmith installed. Hopefully, this keeps Chris out of my place. With the bag in my hand, I walk in quietly and wait to see if I hear anything before moving farther in. After a few minutes, I hear nothing and continue walking in.

Ashley and I had too much to drink last night, so I ended up sleeping on her couch. My pink toenails look nice, though. I walk over to the table and set the bag on top and pull the tissue paper out of it. There is a pair of white shorts and a blush pink strapless top inside. I take another look inside to see who they are from, but there is no card. I wanted little attention on myself, so I told no one it's my birthday today. But who could these be from?

My eyes turn to my phone, wondering if I should ask Cruz if these were from him. I was with Ashley all night, so I can't see how she would have dropped them off. The locksmith asked me if I wanted to get a doorbell camera, but I said no. Now I kind of wish I did. I decide not to call Cruz. Since we haven't spoken, I am worried about where the relationship is going. Only the regular good morning, good night texts. I leave the bag behind and head downstairs to begin my day. Ashley and I both got ready together at her house.

June is standing behind the register, putting the cash inside as I approach her from behind.

"Good morning, June." She jumps at the sound of my voice and turns to face me. "Sorry, I didn't mean to scare you. I thought you would hear me coming down."

"I didn't. I was too busy counting the cash." She shuts the cash register. "Any plans today?"

I give her a side-eye, confused. "Yeah, work."

"Isn't it your birthday?" She turns to face me.

"How did you know?"

She rolls her eyes at me. "You work for me. How else would I not know?"

Oh yeah. She makes a good point.

My body trembles from the creak of the door. June notices me shaking and gives me a strange glance. We both turn toward the front and see a lady walking in. I give her a smile and walk over to greet her.

"Good morning. Anything I can help you look for?"

"No, just checking this place out."

"Okay, I'll be around here if you need anything," I say.

"Actually, I'm looking for a Tiffany style Victorian lamp. Do you guys have any of those?"

"Yes, we do. Let me show you where they are." I walk her to the lamp section and switch them on one by one so she can see they work. "These are the ones we have." She's eyeing them all like they're the ugliest things she has seen. "Are these for you?"

"Oh God no. These are not my style."

Okay. Why is she looking at these then?

"My daughter likes the look of antique furniture. She's been looking for a few of these lamps for her house she is remodeling. I don't know where she got this antique look from because I have never liked it."

"Sometimes daughters can differ completely from their parents with no explanation," I say.

She is touching and feeling around all the lamps. She glances at me. "Are you different from your mother?"

Catching me off guard with that question, I try to swallow, which comes out sounding like I took a big gulp of a drink. "Yes, I am," I say with a slight smile.

"Why is that?"

I squeeze my eyebrows together, wondering what she is getting at. She notices my silence and turns toward me. "Sorry, I don't mean to pry or be nosy. I thought I'd ask because I'm still figuring out my daughter."

"I suppose we grow up to be the people we want to be. I don't think her taste is influenced by you, but rather by her."

"You're right. I'll take these two," she says, touching the two she wants.

I pick them up and walk her back over to the counter. "Do you need these shipped?"

She shakes her head. "I drove here."

I take out bubble wrap from the drawer and start wrapping them. "Are you here on vacation?"

"Yes. My husband skydives all around the world and this was his next stop."

"Oh scary. Do you do it?"

"I have, but it's not my thing. A few times is enough for me. Now I have the choice to watch him or explore on my own."

I box both lamps up and ring her up. "I hope your daughter likes her lamps. It was nice talking to you."

"Same here. Have a good day." She turns around and walks out.

I'm closing up the shop when a call comes through my phone. The name on my screen makes both my cheeks rise. "Hi, Grandma! I miss you."

"Happy birthday to you, happy birthday to you, happy birthday, dear Tessa, happy birthday to you."

"Aww, you're so cute. Thank you."

"Hi, honey. How is your birthday going?"

"Good. I'm off work now, grabbing some pizza. I'm thinking of staying in."

"Why all by yourself?"

"I don't know. Sounds like something I need." I walk around and shut off all the lights. June went home early, so I'm closing up by myself.

"Is everything okay, sweetie?"

"Yes, Grandma. Don't worry. It sounds good to relax tonight."

I've been wanting to try a pizza place a few blocks away. While walking toward there, I continue talking with my grandma and grandpa. My grandma put my grandpa on the phone, but he's such a quiet man. He doesn't say much, only I love you and miss you. I chuckle a lot when I talk to him. He's a man of few words, but the sweetest man I have ever known. I end the call with my grandparents as I'm about to walk into the pizza place. My phone rings and it's Ashley.

"Hi," I say, waiting outside while I take her call.

"What are you doing? Are you off work?"

"Yeah, I'm off. About to pick up my dinner."

"By yourself?"

Why does everyone think it's weird to do stuff by yourself? "Yes."

"I'm outside your place. I thought I could catch you before you were off."

I turn back around and face the way I came as if I'm going to see her, but I'm too far to see anyone over there. "Do you want to have pizza with me?" I ask.

"No. Um..."

Why is she being so hesitant? "Um, what?"

"Can you just come over here? I want to get dinner with you, but I don't feel like pizza. You know what? Stay where you are. I'm coming to get you." She hangs up on me.

I let out a sigh. I really wanted a night to myself. Have a bottle of wine with pizza and take a bubble bath. That's something I haven't done in a while. I just realized I can't take a bath. My studio doesn't have one. Sighing again, I lean my back against the wall, letting people pass by me.

I hear a honk and see Ashley pulled over in front of me. "Hi," I say as I get into her car. She stays quiet and drives off. "Where are we going?" I look over at her. She's gripping the steering wheel like she's nervous about something.

"Can you just trust me?"

I give her a dead stare. "You know?"

"Know what?" she says.

"What today is?"

Both of her eyebrows rise. "What's today?" she says, not facing me as she keeps her eyes on the road.

The rest of the drive to Cruz's house is silent. I caught on to where she was taking me a couple of minutes into the drive. Maybe she really doesn't know it's my birthday. Are Ashley and Cruz going to discuss the argument June just had to tell them about? Oh great. Is this a setup? We pull up to Cruz's house and park. There are no cars outside except for his truck and now

Ashley's car. The pit of my stomach aches. I'm nervous about what's coming. If I were Ashley, I would do the same thing she's doing to me if she were dating my best friend.

"What are we doing here?" I ask.

"Let's go in," she mumbles.

We both slide out of her car and walk up to the house. With every step we take to the front, the pit growing in my stomach increases. I didn't plan on doing this today. Ashley grabs the door handle and opens it. I follow her in and stop in my tracks when I see the house filled with pink and white daisies. What the fuck? Ashley notices I'm not following her. She takes a couple of steps back, grabs my hand, and pulls me toward her. Her face lights up when she sees me confused.

"Come on."

Shocked at what I'm seeing, I stay quiet and follow her in. They filled the island with hors d'oeuvres. She pulls me closer to her as she opens the sliding door, lets go of my hand, and steps out. I stand still, eyes wide, as everyone looks at me. Everyone's mouths are moving, but the sound of their voices is silent, like I've gone deaf. I look back over at Ashley and she gives me a concerned look. My vision is now blurry from the tears that are coming up. What the fuck? Is all I can think.

CHAPTER TWENTY-TWO

Tessa

MY GRANDMA GRASPS my hand as I look down at her and wrap her in a hug. The smell of her hits me and I pull her in closer. My chest shakes and the tears are pouring out.

"Honey, what's wrong?"

I bury my head between her neck and shoulder so no one sees my tears. At this point, everyone knows I'm crying. "I missed you." Another pair of arms wraps around both of us. I don't have to look to know those arms. My grandpa kisses the side of my cheek. After a few minutes, we let go and I wipe the tears away, trying to hide the fact that I was crying, but I'm sure my eyes are now red.

"How did you guys get here?" I say, looking between both my grandparents. My grandma backs away from me and I see Cruz approach all three of us.

"He's a keeper," my grandma says with a wink.

"You did this?" I say to Cruz.

"Yes. I hope it's okay?"

I wrap my arms around him. "Yes, it's more than okay."

He kisses the top of my head. "Then why are you crying?"

I reach for his lips and give him a soft kiss. "I'm so happy. No one has ever done anything like this for me. But how did you get in contact with my grandparents?"

"Well, since I didn't have their number, I saw a letter you had written to them with their address on it. So I wrote them, asking them to call me."

I look back and notice my grandparents took a seat next to June and Cruz's mom. Now I know why June left early to get over here. But I'm still surprised she even came. She has such a big heart.

"Are you happy?"

"Yes, very. I'm just still in shock."

He lets me go and I make my rounds, saying hi to everyone. Even Cheri is here, which I didn't know they knew I knew her. There isn't much introduction I have to do. Everyone is already chatting away.

I sit here, picking at all the food that was made, watching everyone talk. My heart is so full right now. I never thought I would find someone like Cruz or the friends I've made here. Living in a small town has its benefits. Everyone becomes close. Whenever people say everyone knows everyone, I thought they meant it in a bad way. Maybe they mean it like this.

I'm pulled out of my thoughts when I see my grandma glancing at me. The sides of her lips rise upward and a glimmer in her eyes shines as she looks at me. Nothing beats the love between a grandchild and their grandparents.

"When do you and Grandpa go home?" I ask.

"The day after tomorrow."

"Are you ready to go? I'm tired," my grandpa says to my grandma.

She rolls her eyes at him. "I guess we better go. It's past your grandpa's bedtime."

I hug both of my grandparents and walk them out to the front door. Cruz follows behind me and gives them a hug. My stomach forms butterflies watching him hug them. In such a short amount of time, they seem closer than Chris has ever become with them.

Cruz and I walk out to the front porch and take a seat on his swinging chair as we both watch my grandparents drive away. "Are you happy?" Cruz asks.

I lean my head on his shoulder and wrap one of my arms around his. "Very. Thank you for this."

"Ashley said you were trying to go home to have pizza by yourself tonight?"

I chuckle. "Yes. I was."

"Why by yourself?"

"It sounded nice to have a quiet night, with a glass of wine with pizza and take a bubble bath. But then I remembered I don't have a bathtub."

"So then I didn't ruin your night?"

"No. I can have that type of night any day. This surprise topped everything." I tilt my head up and reach for a kiss. He leans in and kisses me. I turn my body a little more toward him as he lifts my legs to lie on his lap. Our breathing is becoming heavier in such a short amount of time. I reach up and wrap my arms around his neck, bringing him closer to me. Until we're both startled by the sound of someone clearing their voice.

Janet, Cruz's mom, is looking at us. "Everyone is heading out. I wanted to say goodbye. I guess our timing is right, given what I walked in on."

Cruz cuts her off. "Mom!"

"What, son? You act like I don't know what's about to happen."

"Okay, stop!" he exclaims.

I rise from my seat and hug her. "Thanks for coming. You raised such a sweet man," I say, as we both look over at Cruz.

"He is a sweetheart."

We both say our goodbyes to everyone else and watch everyone leave.

"Wait here," Cruz says and walks into the house before I can say anything.

About ten minutes later, he comes back out, grabs my hand, and leads me inside. "What did you do now?"

We both walk into his bathroom as he ignores my question. He steps aside and I see he filled his jetted tub up. Some flowers that were around his house are arranged around the tub.

"Sorry, I had no bubbles to put in there."

"It's perfect," I say.

"I'll let you get undressed."

"You're not going to get in?" I ask while taking off my clothes.

"You said earlier you wanted a quiet night alone. At least you can have a quiet bath alone."

As I approach him, I unbutton his shirt and pull it over his head, then unbutton his pants and pull them down to his feet. He takes a step out of his pants and looks down at me while I glance up. My gaze moves down his chest to the bulge that is expanding by the second. I reach up and grab his boxers, pulling them down; the moment his boxers release his cock, it springs up. My palm runs down the shaft of his cock, his veins pulsing. I kneel and swirl my tongue around his head, massaging his balls with one hand while moving up and down his shaft with the other. As I speed up the movement, he lets out a deep breath. I wrap my hands around his ass and press him deeper into the back of my throat. He clenches his fists around my hair and begins fucking my mouth. His heavy breathing has changed into moans.

He pulls my head back and stops me from moving. I gaze up at him. "This is your birthday. I should please you." He lifts me off the ground, squeezes my cheeks, pulls me toward him, and kisses me deeply. He runs his fingers up and down my vagina, rubbing my clit. Quiet moans arise from my throat.

"Let's get in the tub," he says.

He enters the tub first, then spreads his legs in front of him. I get in, straddling him. He leads his cock toward my center. Once he reaches it, I slowly work my way down. I move my hips back and forth while arching my back. I speed up the rhythm a little when my body temperature rises and my center tenses. Cruz's shoulders are my only support as I ride him harder and faster, as my body trembles and my orgasm bursts. My breathing becomes heavy as I try to catch my breath. I rest my head on Cruz's shoulder as I move up and down and finish him. After that, we stayed up all night enjoying each other.

CHAPTER TWENTY-THREE

Tessa

JUNE LET me have a couple of days off since I worked on my birthday. She told me before she left Cruz's the night of my birthday that it was my birthday gift from her. I thought her birthday gift was her showing up last night.

I'm walking back home from the brewery. This morning, Cruz only had eggs to eat, so we headed over to make steak, eggs, and mimosas. Employees started arriving for their shift just as we finished eating, causing Cruz to have to get to work. I wanted to get some fresh air outside, so I walked home.

My legs are a little sore from last night. It feels like I worked them out all night. I guess in a way I did. We stayed up all night and hardly slept. We had sex in his bed and the dining room table after doing it in the bathtub. I told him I've never done it that many times in one night and he said he hadn't either. We were both surprised.

I'm surprised I found a man like Cruz. Someone to go to

sleep with and wake up to eat homemade meals together. It was never like that with Chris. He worked the night shift, so I was always going to bed alone. I would wake up with him in bed, but it's not the same when you both wake up together, start breakfast, sit down, and eat together. Half the time, he was out with friends or heading to work while I started dinner. I ate alone most nights. You realize how little you had once you have more. That's how I feel about Cruz. I thought I was happy with everything I had with Chris. Until I'm now realizing the short time I've had with Cruz is more than I've ever had with Chris.

Chris could easily hang out with a friend since all his friends were single. Looking back, he spent a lot of time with them. I never stopped him from going out. We had our occasional date nights and nights at home together. But he spent most of his time with his friends. Did he start hanging out with the wrong crowd at one point and I never knew? I still can't figure out why he started on drugs.

The moment I round the street to go home, fatigue grips my entire body. My shoulders sag as I walk up the steps to my studio.

"What do you want now?" I say. I'm too tired to deal with this. He's becoming more of a pest rather than an ex. I watch as he stands up. He seems to be bothered by something with his body twitching.

"Did you get my present?" Chris says.

"What present?"

"I left it here the other day on top of the stairs. In a white bag."

I raise my palms to my forehead and shake my head in misery. "Why would you get me something and why can't you leave me alone?"

"It was for your birthday. Every time I came by, you weren't home. I've been sitting out here all morning. Where have you been?" he says while pacing back and forth.

"Are you on something?"

He stops and looks at me dead in the eye. "You always think bad of me. Why do you always think bad of me? I was trying to do something nice. No one can ever accept anything nice from me."

He's not the person I used to know. It's unbelievable what drugs can do to someone in such a short amount of time. It took me a while to understand what was happening when I saw my mom going through this. I know the signs now. He can't act like I don't know. He has lost so much weight and he looks ghostly white. His behavior is so erratic and agitated it's hard to keep up with what's coming next. Not to mention his dilated pupils.

"Why won't you leave me alone? There is nothing for you here. I left for a reason to get away from your dumb ass."

He stops dead in his tracks and looks over at me. "I'm going to get an apartment here so we can be closer together and we can start over. A fresh start," he says with a big grin.

My eyes become blurry from the tears that are coming out. He's going to ruin everything I built for myself here. My job, my relationships. Cruz. A tear falls down my cheek. "Please don't, Chris." I reach my hand up to my face and wipe the tears away. "I want to be happy. Why can't you let me be happy?"

Chris walks over to me and reaches for my hands. I quickly pull away and step back. "I can make you happy. Me!" he says while pointing at his chest.

"I want nothing to do with you. Leave me the fuck alone!" I yell.

Good thing we're in the back of the building where no one is around. It's a small parking space for two cars. Usually mine and June's when she's here working.

"Give me a chance. You'll see. We can get back to how we used to be. No, we can be better. I promise you."

I watch as he backs away from me and walks away. He doesn't turn his back to me until he's a blur in the distance. I look up at the stairway that leads to my studio. I'm hesitant to go in. It doesn't feel like home. Nothing has felt like home since moving in with Chris. My grandparents' house was the only place I considered home. Everywhere I lived, I tried so hard to make it a home for myself. But that feeling never came. Like they say, *Home is where the heart is*. My heart was never with Chris. Now that I'm saying it out loud, I look back at the feeling I had when we lived together. The comfort of living with him never felt comfortable. As far as I can remember, my parents' house was never a home either.

I take my time walking up the steps. Once I'm at the top, I type in the code to my lock and walk into the little square I call home now. Tears fall from my eyes again. Images of me and Cruz going to bed together and waking up together run through my head. *Cruz.* I say to myself. I walk over to my bathroom and turn the shower on. Once my clothes are off, I look at myself in the little round mirror that is above my sink. Black mascara runs down my face. Redness from crying appears on my cheeks. I turn around and enter the shower to wash away yesterday.

After I'm done showering and getting myself ready to help ease the pain from the earlier interaction I had with Chris, I decide to find somewhere to go. I step outside, deciding what to do. I don't want to be alone, but everyone I know is working. Well, I only know two people here. I look down at the last step Chris was sitting on when I came home earlier. I hope he doesn't find a place here. Is there anyone who can stop him from finding a place here? Cruz knows everyone in town, but if I tell him, that means I'm going to have to tell him everything. I'm not ready for that yet. Once I reach the last step of the stairs, I decide to walk around, but instead of walking down Main Street, I walk behind it. I don't feel like running into anyone right now.

CHAPTER TWENTY-FOUR

"HI, FOR HOW MANY?" the hostess asks. After walking around, I found an outside plaza I hadn't seen before. There are a few restaurants, a salon, and this bar I stopped at called Sky Bar.

"Just one." I look around and notice that the area isn't particularly large. Almost no one is at the bar on my right, and empty tables line the left. In the background, there is soft music playing. There aren't many people here. I must have missed the lunch rush. "Could I sit at the bar?"

"Of course. Sit wherever you want," she says and points to the bar.

I give her a small grin and begin walking over there. This is an adorable small spot with plenty of natural light streaming in through the top. When I glance up at the roof, I discover it's made of glass. The barstools are black with gold-plated legs. I slide myself onto the barstool. They covered the entire wall in front of me with booze bottles.

"What can I get you?" the bartender asks.

"I'm not sure." I reach for the menu and open it up to the dessert page. There is a double fudge chocolate cake slice that looks good. "Can I get a slice of your chocolate cake and do you make espresso martinis?"

"Sure do. The martini and cake go well together."

"Let's do that."

I sit and watch as he makes my drink right in front of me.

"Is there anything you're celebrating or just out for a drink and dessert?" He glances at me.

"It's my day off, and I wanted to get out." I don't like attention to myself, so I decide against telling him it was my birthday yesterday.

"It's always nice to have a day for yourself." He sets down my drink. "I'll be back with your dessert."

I lift my drink to my lips and take a little sip. Right away I taste the espresso, then it settles with the taste of the vodka. I haven't had one of these in forever. I forgot how good it was.

"Here you go. How do you like the martini?"

I look down at the cake slice that is much bigger than I expected.

"It's great. Thank you."

"You bet. Let me know if you need anything else."

He walks over to the guy a few seats down from me. I didn't notice him come in. He has a prominent jaw with a shadow of dark brown hair growing around his lower cheek and jawline.

The sweet richness of the cake hits my palate as I take a bite. I wash it down with a sip of my martini. *Oh God, this is good.* This is what I needed. A relaxing day for myself. The soft music coming from the speakers with the mix of alcohol helps set the mood. The blue sky and white clouds catch my eye as I look up at the glass roof. A bird sits on the roof before flying away as another bird swoops past. No wonder this place is called Sky Bar.

"Are you enjoying the view?"

My body jumps from the unexpected voice coming to the right side of me. The guy who was down a few seats is now beside me, holding a draft beer.

"Sorry. Didn't mean to startle you," he says.

"Oh. It's okay. I was too focused on the sky." I chuckle and watch him look above his head.

"That is one beautiful sky."

I take another sip of my martini and watch as he leans back and looks over at me. "I'm Brayden."

He reaches his hand out to mine, and I reciprocate the shake. "I'm Tessa."

"So, Tessa, what brings you here this afternoon?"

"I wanted to get out for the day. What about you?"

"Came to town to visit a buddy of mine. But he doesn't know I'm here, so shhh. Don't say anything." He gives me a wink.

I laugh. "Oh, I won't." I reach my hand up to my lips and pretend like I'm zipping my mouth closed and throwing away the key. He laughs while taking a sip of his beer. "I'm new to town anyway, so I don't know many people here. So your secret is safe with me. Literally."

"What brought you here?"

"I wanted to try somewhere new and landed here. Did you use to live here?"

"For a short while. I never stay in one place for too long and can't with my job."

"Oh really. What do you do?"

"I'm a tour guide for people who want to travel around the world for hiking, backpacking, and camping. Stuff like that. I'm like a travel agent for the wilderness."

His tall, slender frame catches my eye. He must have a lot of stamina, having a job like that.

"What do you do?" He must catch me staring at him as he raises his eyebrows back at me.

"Right now, I work at an antique shop. It's actually called Antique Shop."

"Clever name," he says. "How do you like it here so far?"

"It's nice and hot as hell. I haven't explored much or hiked the red rocks yet."

"What! You need to at least hike the arches. Especially before the sun sets. It's the prettiest time watching the sky turn more red from the reflections of the red rock."

"You have me sold. I'll definitely do that now."

Talking to Brayden has been helpful in taking my mind off things. He goes more into detail about his job and how active it keeps him. Since he's always away, it's been hard for him to settle down with someone. But talking to him makes my mind wander to Cruz and wonder what he's doing or how he feels about us. We haven't talked much about us. Obviously, there is something there since we keep hanging out. I just hope I'm not blindsided by another person.

I'm struggling to finish my cake and notice Brayden keeps looking at it when I take a bite. Is it weird if I ask a stranger if he wants a piece? I'm done with it and it would be a shame for it to go to waste.

"Do you want a bite?" I say.

He gives me a side-eye. "You didn't poison it. Did you?"

"No." I giggle. "I'm done with it. I didn't want it to go to waste. So you can have it."

I watch as he peels a small piece off with his fingers. I guess I should have gotten him another fork.

"This is really good. I'm not much of a dessert guy but this," he says and points to the cake. "Mmm." He drinks the rest of his beer and sets it down. "It was nice talking to you. But I better get going. I need to meet a few people before I surprise my buddy."

He waves down the bartender.

"You want to close your tab?"

"Yes. And put hers on mine," he says.

"No. You don't have to do that."

"It's the least I can do since I interrupted your day." He hands the bartender his card.

"You didn't interrupt my day. I enjoyed our conversation."

"Will you let me take you out to dinner and we can continue this?" he says with a grin on his face.

My cheeks warm up. If it wasn't for Cruz, I would say yes.

"With that hesitation and bright red cheeks, I can already tell there is someone else?" he says.

"There is someone. It's new, so not sure where it's heading, but I would like to see what comes of it."

"With that cheerful grin on your face, I can tell you really like him. He's a lucky guy." He signs his receipt and puts his card back into his wallet.

I touch my cheeks and realize they are warmer than I expected. Especially since this bar has AC.

"I hope things work out between you two." He steps off the barstool.

"So do I. Thank you for paying for me. It was actually my birthday yesterday, so that's part of the reason I'm here. I had the day off and didn't want to sit at home by myself." I'm guessing the alcohol gave me the courage to let someone know.

"Oh nice. Happy birthday, Tessa."

He reaches in for a hug. As I hug him back, I say, "Thank you."

"I hope you enjoy the rest of your day. Take care."

"You too," I say and watch as he walks away and heads out the door.

CHAPTER TWENTY-FIVE

Tessa

I HOP on the swing that hangs from Cruz's porch and sway myself back and forth. After Brayden left, I had more drinks at the bar. Once the dinner rush started picking up, I left. I went for a walk and found a park to hang out at before deciding to go to Cruz's place. I thought about going to the brewery, but they were about to close and I didn't want to be in the way.

I've gone back and forth, wondering if I should talk to Cruz about us and what he's feeling. It's pretty obvious how we both feel, but with my luck, you never know. Should I even further this relationship since I still haven't told him about stupid Chris? Or wait until Chris gets the hint and leaves me alone? I doubt he will. Plus, who wants to deal with a girl and her ex-boyfriend? That's another reason why I'm so hesitant. And Chris sounds pretty determined, even though he's not in his right state of mind. You never know what's coming next with him.

The sound of tires pulling up the driveway causes butterflies to flutter in my stomach. Cruz's headlights shine in my direction, making it impossible for me to see him in his truck. I hear two doors open and close before the lights go out. I raise my arm to my forehead to check who he's with. Ashley appears in the distance.

I stand up and reach for a hug. "Hi."

"Hey! What are you doing? I didn't see your car."

"I walked over here."

She squints her eyebrows. "Why did you walk? It's kind of far."

"I don't know. I spent the evening walking around and then came here."

"Hey, handsome," I say as I walk into Cruz's arms.

"Handsome? I like it," he says. "What are you doing here?"

I step back and glance between Cruz and Ashley. "Why is everyone so surprised I'm here?"

"That was my boss. He found another lead." He stops mid-sentence when he sees me. "Oh, hey, Tessa. Long time no see."

"Hi, Brayden," I say in a surprised tone. What is he doing here?

Cruz looks between me and Brayden. "Do you two know each other?"

"Ugh, we met earlier today at Sky Bar. Is this the guy you are seeing?" Brayden says and points to Cruz.

I nod.

"What's going on?" Cruz asks.

"Oh, nice," Brayden says and pats Cruz on the back. "He's a keeper."

A big grin forms on my face. "I know."

We're all on the porch, looking at each other. Ashley has stayed quiet this whole time.

"Is someone going to fill me in?" Cruz asks again.

"We met at Sky Bar. She was alone, and I was alone, so we started talking. One thing led to another."

My face drops and I look up at Cruz. His eyes are wide, brows raised.

"I'm fucking with you, man. We only talked. I asked her out, and she turned me down. She said there was someone else in her life." He winks over at me. "If I knew it was you, I would have put in a good word for you."

I laugh. "I already know he's a good guy."

Cruz looks over at me and smiles. "I guess there is no need for introductions then."

"Is this the buddy you were surprising?" I ask Brayden.

"Sure is."

We all head inside, and Ashley makes us drinks. She's always creating mixed drinks. Makes me wonder why she isn't a bartender. I watch as she cuts cantaloupe into pieces and places it into a blender to make a puree.

"Can you cut this cucumber into slices?" She pulls one out of a grocery bag and hands it to me.

"Yeah." I grab the cucumber and head over to the sink to wash it. "What are you making now?"

"Something I found on the internet. You'll see."

I sit back down and start cutting the cucumber. I watch her pour a cup of the puree into a cocktail shaker and shake in a few shots of cucumber vodka. She gets two glasses, fills them halfway with ice, and pours sparkling water into the glasses. She divides the vodka and puree evenly between both of our glasses. Then she tops it off with a few cucumbers. I throw straws into the cup and we both reach up and clink our glasses together.

"Mmm, this is good. You should become a bartender."

I look outside over Ashley's shoulder and see Cruz and Brayden in a deep conversation. Was there a reason for Brayden's return besides just stopping by?

Ashley turns and sees what I'm looking at. "Let's go outside."

I follow her out, and both of them go silent. Their silence makes it sound like they were talking about us.

My arms wrap around Cruz's neck as I sit on his lap. "I missed you." To my surprise, he stays quiet and says nothing back. That's odd. I release my arms and glance at Brayden, who stares at us with wide eyes. An uneasy feeling settles down my body with Cruz's demeanor and the way Brayden looks at us. I get off Cruz and take a seat next to him.

Everything is off tonight. They are busy catching up on their lives, so no one else seems to notice.

"When are you going to settle down, Brayden?" Ashley asks.

He looks over at me first before answering Ashley's question. Weird.

"I'm too busy with work to settle down. I'm always on the go."

"All you and Cruz do is work. I'm actually surprised he started something with Tessa," she says and everyone looks over at me.

Eyes wide, I look over at Cruz. "You really didn't date a lot?"

"No," Ashley answers for him.

"I told you I didn't," Cruz says.

"Isn't that what most men say when they are trying to get a girl?" I question.

"Why do girls always turn our words upside down?" We all turn our attention back over to Brayden. "Some things are simply said, but it's taken completely different."

"Shut up, Brayden! There was a time when you were a man whore and said all kinds of things to girls," Ashley exclaims.

"Yeah, but that was when I was young and dumb."

"Some men stay young and dumb forever," I say.

Ashley bursts out laughing. I look over at her, biting my bottom lip to stop myself from laughing. Both Cruz and Brayden shake their heads, not amused by us one bit.

The conversation continues to flow and every once in a while, they ask me a question. Probably so I don't feel left out. Which is nice because it helps me feel included. The way Cruz's demeanor changed the second these two spent time alone on the porch has me overthinking. Is he mad Brayden asked me on a date? I turned him down. There is nothing to be mad about.

"How long are you in town for?" Ashley asks Brayden.

"It's looking longer than I expected."

"Do you have a tour you have to do?" I ask.

"A tour?" Ashley blurts out.

"Yeah. Remember, I'm a wilderness tour guide," he says with an intensified glare, as if he's trying to make her play along.

"Oh, that's right. That was a blonde moment." She chuckles and slaps herself lightly on her forehead.

They both have grins on their faces, ignoring what just happened as I watch.

"Where's your tour?" I ask.

Brayden clears his throat. "At Dead Horse State Park."

"Oh, where is that?" I say and notice Ashley's furrowed eyebrows. I glance at Cruz and his face is expressionless. He doesn't acknowledge me. I know he sees me.

"It's about thirty miles from here." He lifts himself higher on the chair, almost squirming as if he's uncomfortable with this conversation.

"Are you going on a hike?"

He nods as he rests his elbow on the chair and leans his head into his hand.

I end my questions there, wondering why everything still feels so off. The rest of the night goes smoother. I listen to Cruz explain how his brewery is going. It was nice to learn about it since I didn't know much. When we're together, he doesn't like to talk about work. He likes to leave work behind once he leaves. Which he can now do since he has put his time in to get it up and running and has employees who help run the place.

I stand and glance at Ashley. "Do you want a refill?"

"No, I think I'm done for the night. It's actually getting late. I should head out."

Everyone follows suit and I watch as everyone says their goodbyes. I wave to Brayden and Ashley as I clean up around the kitchen. Cruz walks back in and helps me with the rest of the stuff.

"Is everything okay between us?" I ask.

He shuts the fridge and looks over at me. "Yes. Why wouldn't it be?"

"Something feels off."

"Like what?" He comes over to me and pulls me into his warm arms.

"I don't know. Like you're mad or bugged at me about something." I wrap my arms around him as much as I can.

"It was a long day at work. Let's go to bed." He walks us both into his room. He pulls one of his T-shirts out of his drawer and hands it to me. Then heads to the bathroom.

My plan to talk to him about us is going to have to wait. Something must be on his mind. I don't want to throw more stuff at him in case it stresses him out even more. I head to the bathroom outside his room and splash water on my face. Once I get back to his room, he's already in bed. As I open the covers and slide into the side I usually sleep on, I roll over to face him. He appears deep in thought while staring up at the ceiling. I guess nothing is going to happen tonight. Not even talking.

"Is there anything you want to talk about?" I ask.

He shakes his head.

"Okay, well, I'm here if you need to talk."

"Okay," he says.

"Good night."

"Night, Tessa."

CHAPTER TWENTY-SIX

I EXITED the Pizza Parlor with lunch for both June and myself. June eats so healthy. She ordered a salad and one breadstick. Meanwhile, I went for a small pizza with everything on it. I'm sure that's why she's in such great shape for her age.

This morning was busy for us. We received a huge shipment of antiques. We had to carry them off the truck and put them into the back room, all while still helping customers in between. The truck drivers always do it, but this one said he was behind schedule and asked us to help. I feel bad when she helps unload the truck, so she mostly helps customers. And she rarely argues about that when I tell her I got it. She seems to be getting tired of this job but doesn't want to let it go. It's all she has known her whole life. I'm sure it makes it hard.

While balancing the food on my other hand, I cautiously open the shop door and slowly make my way to the back.

"Excuse me," I say to the man blocking my way to the backroom.

He turns around. "Oh. I'm sorry."

"Brayden? What are you doing here?" I set the food on the counter, even though June hates when we have food out on the floor. She always tells me she specifically made a backroom for us to eat at.

"I came to say hi to June. You know, making my rounds," he says with a grin.

It's been a few days since I've seen him, so I thought he left already for one of his tours. Cruz nor Ashley have said anything about him. I'm still trying to get a read on him. He rubbed me the wrong way after the night at Cruz's house. I haven't brought it up to anyone because I hardly know him and don't feel like I should yet.

"No food on the counter," June exclaims.

As I glance behind me, I see June approaching. "I know. Sorry. I was saying hi to Brayden." I pick up the food and head to the backroom before I get scolded like a child. When I return up front, Brayden is hugging June goodbye.

"It was nice seeing you, Tessa."

"You're leaving already?"

"Yeah, I got some business I need to take care of. I'll see you around, though. I'll be staying here a little longer."

"Okay. See ya later." I turn to June but notice she has already gone to the backroom. I make my way to the back, trying to get out of the maze we built with the shipment. "How do you know Brayden?" I ask her and grab a slice of pizza.

"He grew up here and when you live here, you know everyone."

I nod as I chew a slice of pizza down before a customer comes in. I skipped breakfast this morning. I'm extra hungry.

"So are you ever going to tell me your story?"

That's a weird question from June, especially right after

Brayden left. She hasn't seemed to care to get to know me. "What story?"

"Don't act dumb with me, missy. Everyone has a story."

"What's yours?" She's not one to tell anyone her life story either, so why the sudden interest in mine?

"You know my story."

I give her a side-eye. "I do?"

She sets her fork down, grabs a drink of water, and then dabs her lips with a napkin. "Born and raised here. Helped my parents run this shop until I took it over. Never married. That's it. That's me."

That's not a story, so I decide to give her the same version she gave me. "My grandparents raised me. Moved here to find something new. I found a job with you. That's it. That's me."

She shakes her head. "Smart-ass."

I chuckle, trying to hold in the piece of my pizza I shoved in my mouth. I didn't expect that from her. The creaks from the door catch us off guard. "I'll get it." I stand up and wipe my mouth off and head over to help the customer.

In the corner, I see a man looking at the old leather wallets we have. "Hi, can I help you with anything?" The second those words came out of my mouth, I recognized who it is.

"How much is this?" he says with a smirk on his face.

"What are you doing here?" I whisper. The last thing I want is for June to know who he is. I grab the wallet out of his hand and set it back down. "You need to leave." I try pushing him toward the door so I can shove him out. Since I'm trying not to make a scene, I don't use all my force on him and he's not budging. "Chris, you have to leave. I work here."

"No. We need to talk."

"No. We don't. You need to get the hell out of my life." I don't get him. He shows up out of nowhere, then he's a ghost, and then he shows up again. I don't see how he thinks any of this will make me want him back. Every time he disappears, I pray he doesn't come back. Then days or weeks go by and he shows up again.

"I found an apartment that I move into in a few weeks. I can help you pack your stuff until it's ready."

I give him a blank look and quit pushing him. "What the fuck are you talking about? Are you delusional? I don't want to see you ever again, let alone live with you."

His eyebrows rise as if I told him devastating news. "How are we going to work things out if you don't move in with me?"

"There is nothing to work out. I don't want to be with you. How many brain cells have you fried?"

I'm about to push him again but stop when another customer walks in. I stand up a little straighter and smile at her. "Hi, let me know if you have questions," is all I can mutter.

"Chris! Please leave. You can't do this at my job," I whisper, trying to keep my composure.

"I promise we can make this work. Come on, it's me."

I hear footsteps in the distance and see June walking over to the customer, eyeing us. I smile a little to show everything is all right.

"And we need to start furniture shopping."

"What! No. I'm not living with you. You don't even have a job. How the hell do you expect to buy furniture? With my money?"

"Well, since we're together, it's our money."

Fuck, he's more delusional than I thought. The best thing I've learned to not make situations like this bigger is to play along. "Okay. We'll talk after I'm off work."

A big smile forms on his face. "Okay, when do you get off?"

"Eleven," I say. We close at eight, but that at least gives me a three-hour window before he's out looking for me. I pray he goes off and gets high somewhere and forgets.

"Eleven? That seems too late to keep this shop open."

"Well, I have closing responsibilities that need to get done before I can leave."

He goes back toward the door. I sigh and feel my shoulders release the tension they were holding.

"Okay, I'll see you at eleven."

It takes everything in me not to slam the door in his face. I make sure he leaves while watching him walk away through the window. Another customer comes in and I jump from the creaking noises.

June and I were able to get everything from the shipment unpacked and out on the floor by closing. I'm glad because all day I've been jumpy, expecting Chris to walk back through those doors. I was expecting June to ask who he was, but she hadn't. She kept to herself the rest of the day.

After we closed the shop, I packed a small overnight bag and raced over to Cruz's house. I brought my car in case Chris returned and noticed my car parked outside, assuming I'm at home. I don't have a plan, so I figured I could surprise Cruz when he got home from work. I hope he's alone and that I don't mess with his plans. When I get to his place, I see he's already there. When I approach the door, I slow down to hear if anyone is there. There are no sounds inside, so he must be alone. I'm standing in front of the door, unsure of what to do. Should I enter? I'm hesitant about what to do. This is why I've been wanting to talk to Cruz about us.

I choose to ring the doorbell and hear footsteps on the other side. The door opens and I look up at Cruz's confused face. "Hey," I mutter. I'm not sure if he's confused that I rang the doorbell or that I'm here.

"Why didn't you walk in?"

"I didn't know if it was okay to." That answers my question. He opens the door wider and that same warm apple scent fills my nostrils.

"You're always welcome here. Come in."

He takes a few steps back, making room for me to walk in. We both walk over to the kitchen and I notice the sun is setting behind his house. It's giving a colorful glow to his pool. "What were you up to?"

"Nothing. I was just thinking."

"Oh," I say. He's quieter today. "Do you want me to go?"

"No. I was going to take a swim. Wanna join?" he says with a wink.

"Sure. But I didn't bring my swimsuit." I turn around and see his shirt is already off and he's unbuttoning his pants.

"Who needs a swimsuit? It's only us."

"Okay, I see where this is heading." I move away from him and walk toward the pool. When I get to the patio, I take off my clothes with my back to him. The cool night breeze strikes my skin, making me shiver. Cruz comes up behind me, wrapping his arms around my stomach and kissing my neck, causing goose bumps to run down my body. His bulge is pressing into my backside. I reach around and stroke his head on my palm in a circular motion. His pre-cum is leaking, making it easier to rub him.

He picks me up and leads me down to the pool, where we sit on the last step. I straddle him, placing my hands over both of his cheeks and leading him in for a kiss. We're both up to our waists in the water. I start to rock my hips, causing my clit to move up and down his shaft. My rocking intensifies as he reaches down and grabs my ass. I hold Cruz's shoulders to keep myself stable as my back arches and my hips rock. The tension in our bodies is rising. Cruz leans in and sucks on my nipple while spinning his tongue over it, which sets me off even more.

My breathing deepens, and my orgasm erupts through my

body. My entire body trembles as I come down from the high and lean against Cruz's chest. I raise my hip and slide his cock inside of me inch by inch, stretching me to his size. I roll my hips up and down, taking him all in. Cruz grabs my hips and pushes me down harder with each movement. Each time, he moans a little harder. After collecting my breath following my orgasm, I'm finally able to speed up my rhythm. I move faster and hear Cruz moan harder than before. I watch as his head slumps back and his fists sink into my hips even more as he releases his orgasm.

CHAPTER TWENTY-SEVEN

Tessa

"IS that all I can get for you?" our waiter asks.

"Yes," Cruz responds.

Cruz planned this special night for us as it's been a while since we have gone on a date together. Things have calmed down and I haven't seen much of Chris around. I'm not even sure whether or not he got the apartment. Every night, I hope he doesn't. I've found something that works for me, and I don't want it to fall apart.

The waiter comes around and opens a bottle of Malbec that Cruz ordered for us. I watch as he pours us each a glass. We came to this fancy steak house called The Cliff Steakhouse. It sits on the edge of a red rock, making it so we can look out into the valley down below.

"Your sesame ginger seared scallops appetizer should be out soon."

"Thank you," I say.

This place is romantic with the dark atmosphere and jazz music playing softly in the background. I notice most people here are couples. At one table, a guy's arm is reached across the table, holding on to his wife's hand, twirling her wedding ring around between his fingers. Are they newlyweds? Have they been married for years and are still madly in love with each other? I've always wished for that. But how can I have that if I can't even be open with the man I'm falling for? I hate Chris for taking my trust away. Now it's making it hard to trust someone else. The one thing I always had for people is trust, even with everything I grew up with. The trust my grandparents gave me helped me open up to others.

"What are you thinking about?" Cruz asks, taking me out of my thoughts.

"Oh umm. I don't know." I want to express my feelings and tell him everything about myself. But what if we don't work out and I put my trust in someone else, only to have my heart destroyed again? Trust comes with a lot of vulnerability, and I'm not sure if I'm there yet. But I don't want to lose him either.

"There is something I've been meaning to talk to you about," Cruz says with a burning look in his eyes. This must be serious. I've never seen that expression on him. He's always laid back and chill around me. That's the one thing I've loved about him. How easy it is to be around him.

"What is it?" I say as I gulp down my wine to help ease my nerves.

"That guy you ran away from in the brewery. Who is he?"

My face flushes with heat. The conversation surprised me. Despite that, I knew it would come up at some point. But because it hadn't for a long time, I assumed Ashley had told him.

"Tessa."

I look up at him.

"I know you're not one to open up, but when you hear stuff going around town, it makes me wonder what's really going on."

"What are you hearing?"

"People have seen you and that guy arguing outside your place a few times. I heard there was an argument in your studio that customers could have heard from the store."

I never considered this, but what if there are cameras in the back of the store that I am clueless about? I know June overheard us arguing and must have told Cruz, but I don't believe anyone saw us outside together. "Who told you about us arguing outside?"

"You can't answer a question with a question. I've been patient enough and I can't keep thinking something is going on, Tessa. I need answers."

"I—" I'm cut off as the waiter brings us our appetizer and a bowl of bread. The food has now lost its appeal to me as I look down at it. *Come on, open up.*

"I don't want to lose you, but I am also not going to be played with," Cruz says as he forks one scallop and pops it into his mouth.

"His name is Chris. He's my ex." I watch Cruz's expression, but it stays the same as it was before, like he's not surprised. I guess he figured that out. He stays silent, waiting for me to go on. "He got into drugs and I left him. That's why I came here to start over. I have a complicated past, and I wanted to start over. A fresh start where no one knows me. I never knew he would find me here. I don't even know how he found me. He's so messed up on drugs, he comes and goes. He'll randomly show up, asking to give him another chance. Then disappear for days or weeks until he shows back up again."

The waiter drops off our steaks, sides, and refills our wine glasses for us. I reach over and take another gulp down. The warmth travels through my throat down to my stomach. I hope it relaxes me more. I didn't even realize I finished the last glass.

"Why couldn't you have told me that?" he asks.

"I wasn't trying to hide anything from you. I just... I have a hard time trusting people now. I've been through a lot and I've always been open with people and being so open has backfired on me in the past, making it hard to trust anyone now."

"What else have you been through?" he says, while serving portions of mac and cheese and asparagus to each of us. I guess he realized I haven't touched any of the food and is trying to make me eat.

"Can we take one step at a time and not go down that conversation yet?"

He gives me a side-eye and nods.

"Cruz, I promise I'll open up to you. I want to trust more. All I need is more time," I say.

"How do I know in time you'll trust me enough to open up to me? I had to come to you about your ex."

"Because I like you a lot and I want to see where this takes us. I know opening up to one another is what helps relationships grow, but I need more time. Can you give me more time?" He stays silent, looking beyond me. "Cruz." He brings his gaze back to me. "How do you feel about us? Do you not want to continue this?"

"Yes, I do. That's why I'm questioning what the hell is going on with you. I keep thinking we are on the right track, but then I hear things and it makes me think maybe it's all in my head. I didn't even know what you wanted between us until right now," he says and takes a sip of his wine.

"Have my actions not shown you that I like you and want something with you?"

"They do, but then I hear something. Then I get all in my head and question everything."

"Please don't question my feelings for you." My eyes sting from the tears that are building up. I didn't want this to happen. I was afraid it might, and now that it has, I feel like Cruz is hanging on by a thread. How could I be so stupid to think he wouldn't find out? This is a small town. Everyone knows everyone. This isn't fair. I deserve to be happy without my past haunting me.

"How is everything?" the waiter says, eyeing my plate. "Is everything tasting okay? You haven't touched your food."

I look up and wipe the tears away and nod. He gives me a slight smile and walks away.

"Tessa, I didn't mean to make you cry." He leans toward me and grabs my hand and wraps it into his. "I don't want you to cry. I wanted to have a conversation about this to clear the air."

"Trust me when I say nothing is going on with him. You're the only person I've been with since coming here."

"I trust you, but you need to trust me and tell me when he comes back."

I give him a nod and he pulls my hand up toward his mouth and places a kiss on the top.

"Let's enjoy the rest of our dinner."

The rest of the night goes much better. We laugh all night at Cruz's stories about the drunk people he's had to deal with while running a brewery. I'm sure half the drunks assume he's a bouncer. So it's a good thing he's huge and muscular. We finish our food and dessert and return to his house. We're both so full that all we want to do is sit on the back porch with the night sky above us, the air cooling us off after the heat of the day. Simple acts like this make me feel so at ease with him, even without words. Having someone here with you makes you feel like it's only you and the other person in this entire world, and no one can break you apart.

CHAPTER TWENTY-EIGHT

Tessa

I HEAR the crowd in the back roaring and saying *"what the hell"* while we start our way down the Colorado River on our tubes. Cruz knows the owner of the local tubing business that's here in town. He let us have our own private time down the river without a huge crowd following us. So we get to butt in line. Knowing everyone in a small town has many perks I never realized. It seems unfair, but they claim it's a regular thing.

We each have our own tube. Brayden is at the start of the line, holding on to Ashley's tube. Ashley is holding on to my tube and I'm holding on to Cruz, who's in the back.

"Pass me a beer, Ash?" Brayden asks.

Ashley takes a Corona from one of the waterproof drink bags we brought with us. Floating down the river takes a few hours. We packed another bag with food so we could eat lunch at a spot Cruz and Ashley know about. The water is peaceful, opposite to what I expected. When I drive by rivers like these, the water always seems to move too quickly for anyone to get into. I was hesitant when they mentioned tubing down the river. It's pleasant and soothing. We're surrounded by red rock with a few patches of green. Despite no breeze, the water keeps you cool under the sun.

"Do you guys want to get in a circle?" Cruz asks. Everyone nods. Brayden holds on to a rock, stopping us from moving, while Cruz paddles with his hands over to Brayden's tube and grabs a hold of it. Ashley hands Cruz three Coronas so he can open them for us.

"Thank you," I say while grabbing the beer from him.

"Tessa," Ashley says. With her phone up, she's taking a picture of us. I move a little closer to her and smile. "Brayden, since you're in the front, can you get us all in a picture?" She says and hands him her phone. He reaches his arm up with the phone in his hand and takes a few pics.

"Let me see." Ashley and I inspect the photos and decide on the ones we like the most. "Send them to me when you get a chance," I ask.

"I will."

Cruz and Brayden have been more quiet than usual. I can't say how they interact since I haven't been around them. Ashley hasn't said much either. But she's distracted with the pictures and uploading them to her social media. She asked me once if I had one. I told her no. I actually do, but I haven't been on those apps in a while. I felt like it was junk for my brain and not doing any good for me.

"There is a drop coming up. We should be fine if we keep holding on to each other," Brayden says. He sounds like he guides tours, and he knows what he's doing. "Here it comes."

"Ahhh," I say as we go down the drop. My butt lifts slightly off the tube during the drop. All three of them look at me with their cheeks raised in a laugh they're trying to hold back.

"Are you okay?" Cruz asks.

"Yes. It wasn't that bad. I scared myself by overthinking."

"I told you the river isn't too bad."

"Yeah, it isn't. I'll trust you next time." I smile at Cruz. He gives me a wink. I guess my trust is worse than I thought. I didn't trust any of them when they told me it wasn't bad.

Trust is such a tricky thing. It can be destroyed in an instant and it takes longer to rebuild trust after it has been destroyed.

"These upcoming turns are where there are places to stop at. Let me know where you guys want to stop for lunch," Brayden says.

We come around a corner and see a small piece of land with trees. It almost looks like a little island in the middle of the ocean, but in this case, a river.

I point toward it. "Do you guys want to stop there?"

"Yeah, that looks like a good spot," Ashley says. "I have to pee, too."

Cruz releases Brayden's tube and we paddle with our hands to get closer. Once we're in shallow water, Cruz and Brayden get off their tubes and walk us over there. Ashley and I get out of our tubes when we get to the island and set them on the dirt ground.

"Do you want to come pee with me?" Ashley asks.

"Are there bathrooms?"

She chuckles. "No. You have to pop a squat out here."

"Ah, okay," I mutter.

"Don't tell me you've never peed out in the wilderness?" She leads me farther into the trees and bushes, out of sight.

Once we are out of sight of the guys, I say, "I have, but I wasn't sure how you guys all felt about that. It turns some guys off."

Ashley stops and looks around. "I don't think anyone can see us here." She squats down and starts doing her business. And then I follow the lead away from her so she can't see me. "These guys don't care. Growing up here, you explore the outdoors since that's all there is to do. So where else is a child going to pee when they're in the middle of nowhere?"

"So all three of you grew up together?" I say as we walk back.

"Yeah."

"Have you and Brayden ever had a thing?"

Ashley chuckles. "No. Never. The people I grew up with are like brothers and sisters to me. Why do you ask?"

"I don't know. I can't figure Brayden out."

"What's there to figure out?"

"He's different from the first time we met. After finding out I know you and Cruz, he seems more standoffish with me."

"Hmmm," she says.

I look over at her and she's staring straight ahead like she's trying to avoid this conversation. That's weird. I don't know if I should press more about it or let it go. Maybe it's all in my head because why would he want to hang out with me if he had a problem with me?

We both get back to the guys and I notice they have set up our tubes in a circle with food in the middle lying out on plates. The trees that surround us are giving us a good amount of shade while we eat.

"Here." Ashley hands me a bottle of hand sanitizer. I squeeze some in my hand and then hand it back to her.

"You two set this up so cute," I say, looking between Cruz and Brayden. Brayden's shoving a piece of the sub sandwich into his mouth while nodding. I reach over, grab my plate Cruz made for me and another beer, and start eating. "So, Brayden, have you done tours down this river before?" A gagging sound comes from Brayden right after I asked that.

"Are you okay?" Ashley says.

He nods and takes a sip of his beer. "Went down the wrong tube," he says. "Umm, but yes. I've been down this river before."

"How'd you get into what you do?"

"I sort of fell into it," he says and shrugs his shoulders.

He's a man with not so many words now. He talked so much when we first met. I look over at Ashley and Cruz, and both of them are staying quiet and don't make eye contact with me. Is he a private guy? But he didn't seem so private the first day we met. This makes little sense. Maybe I need to drop it. I can't force a friendship.

After we finish our lunch, we all head back out on the tubes. This time, we get caught up next to other groups of people. All three of them are talking amongst themselves. Cruz will ask me questions here and there. I think only to make me feel included. These three have a long history, so it is easy for them to conversate. Especially since they rarely see Brayden.

"Do you want to spend the night with me?" Cruz asks as we walk back to his truck. The time went by quickly. It felt like we were only out there for a few hours. Once we get back to the truck, my phone shows we had been out there for five hours.

My stomach growls a little. "Can we stop and get takeout? I'm tired now. The sun, beer, and motion of the river relaxed me too much."

"Yeah, it does that to you."

I'm sitting at Cruz's dining table, setting out the pizza while he gets us plates and napkins. After we dropped Ashley and Brayden off, we stopped and got a pizza to go. It was the easiest thing I could decide on. Cruz and I are more beat than we thought. We sit in silence, slowly eating.

"Do you know what sounds good right now?" I say.

"What?"

"A shower, us in your bed cuddling, and watching a movie."

"That sounds perfect," he says, and we both stand up and clean the kitchen.

Our relationship almost seems to have our routine down smoothly. Like when you fall into a routine with your significant other because you've been living together for so long. But not in a bad way.

We returned home, ate, cleaned up the kitchen, showered, and are now wrapped up in bed watching a movie. We both went with the flow, as if we were in rhythm with one other, and then in the morning we woke up, had breakfast, and were both on our way to work. This appeals to me because of its simplicity. Chris was never this simple, and he was never home because he worked evenings. I enjoy relationships in which your significant other is in tune with you throughout the relationship. When you have it, it is something to treasure. The more I think about Chris's and my relationship, the more I realize how far it was from being a relationship.

CHAPTER TWENTY-NINE

IT'S A FRIDAY NIGHT, and Cruz's brewery is hosting a new band. He said they play great and invited me to come over after work to hang out with him. I'm not sure what to wear. It's been a while since I've done a full face of makeup. My usual routine consists of applying mascara and sunscreen, and I'm done. I've been missing it, so I went all out on my makeup tonight. I apply foundation, concealer, contour, highlight, and lip gloss. My high-rise jean shorts look great with the black ankle-strap sandals that extend several inches above my ankles. I'm wearing a black V-neck tank top that shows off my boobs just a little. I take one last look in the mirror before walking out the door.

It's only eleven o'clock when I get to the brewery and it's already packed. I look around for Ashley, but I can't see her at all. Every table and booth are overfilled with people. The band is playing "Nirvana Come As You Are." I instantly start feeling the vibe of the crowd. It's a good vibe with everyone enjoying themselves and the band. I squeeze through everyone to make my way to the back of the bar to see if I can find anyone I know.

Jason spots me and heads my way. "Hey, Tessa," he shouts in my ear, but it doesn't sound that loud with the music blaring over the speakers.

"Hi, where is everyone?" I look around the bar and notice Cruz or Ashley aren't here.

He points to our right, up by the stage where the band is. "They have a table over there. There are so many people, you can't see. But if you head that way, you should find them."

I nod my head.

"Do you want a drink before you head over there?"

"Yes, let's do a vodka soda with extra lime."

"Really? You usually order an IPA."

"I don't feel like drinking heavily tonight. The carbs from the beer are getting to me," I say as I pat my stomach.

He throws his head back and laughs. Once my drink is done, I head over to where Cruz is. It's even harder to get through the people with a drink in my hand. Cruz's back is to me when I spot him sitting with Ashley and Brayden.

I walk up behind Cruz, lean into his ear, and whisper, "Hey, handsome." He turns around and stares me in the eyes. When he realizes it's me, my stomach spins, and a smile spreads across his face. He reaches up and places his hand on my lower back before pulling me into his lap. I place my drink on the table and lean in for a kiss. He softly bites my bottom lip, sucks it, and then releases me. The glare in his eyes is pure hunger for me, and it makes my center ache for him.

"Get a room." I hear Ashley yell.

We both look over at her and watch her laugh at us. I glance over at Brayden's annoyed facial expression. He didn't have that look on his face before I came.

"You look hot, Tess," Ashley yells.

My face lightens up with a smile from ear to ear. "Thanks. I'm surprised Cruz isn't making you work."

"I'm supposed to, but there is nowhere to sit people now." She shrugs her shoulders. "So I'm out of a job tonight."

I nod and Cruz leans into my neck and whispers, "You do look hot tonight. Good thing you're all mine."

"Is that so? I'm all yours?" I whisper.

"You better be."

"Who else's would I be?" I ask.

"I don't know. You tell me."

Before I can answer, he leans back into my neck and begins kissing me. Goose bumps appear on my neck. I turn my head and see Brayden looking at us. But the moment he notices me looking at him, he moves his glare back to the band. I'm curious if Cruz notices how he's acting around me right now. Is he unhappy with Cruz and me together? I clear my mind of all my thoughts. I'm not going to think about what Brayden thinks of me. Or what he thinks of me and Cruz being together. If Cruz hasn't said anything to me, it's possible that this is all in my imagination.

After a few hours, I'm feeling more and more drunk. Cruz asked me to go home with him tonight. Not so much asked, but demanded. He said *drink as much as you want because you're coming home with me tonight so I can have my way with you.* I've been hoping all night he'd take me to his office and have his way with me. I'm betting he doesn't want to do it at his place of business. It's not like he can get in trouble since he owns it. Our business might get out before we can finish, since it's a small town. He probably doesn't want to jeopardize his reputation here.

Cruz and Ashley only had a few drinks at the start of the night but stopped so they're able to close. The crowd is getting smaller as the night is coming closer to an end. As I'm enjoying the band and dancing on Cruz's lap, I notice Brayden looking my way. When I turn my attention toward him, he sits up a little taller in his seat and then I am met with a tap on my shoulder.

"What are you doing?" I hear.

My heart rate drops as rapidly as my blood sugar does. My head is hazy from the dizziness that is rushing in. The hand that tapped me on the shoulder grips my upper arms and pulls me away from Cruz's lap. Cruz jumps up and looks down at Chris, grabbing his wrist and squeezing it until Chris lets go. Cruz's head moves to Brayden, and he gives him a tiny nod. My brows furrow in confusion at what is going on. Brayden stands up and looks at Chris, but he doesn't approach him.

"What are you doing, Tessa? I found us an apartment so we can start a life here and you're over here with someone else."

I look between Cruz and Chris, not sure what to say. Cruz looks dumbfounded by the words that come out of Chris's mouth. "Cruz, it's not true."

"What do you mean, it's not true? We've been with each other every night since I got here." Chris looks up at Cruz. "I'm sorry, man, but it's true. We've been together this whole time. She was with me last night."

"No, I wasn't. I was with him," I say, pointing at Cruz.

"No, you weren't. You said you were tired and wanted to go home after work and get some rest," Cruz says.

I shake my head. It feels so clustered right now. "No, last night we had pizza and then watched a movie in bed."

"That was the night before."

I stand there wide-eyed, trying to remember. The stupid alcohol has my days and nights all mixed up.

"See, you were with me last night."

"Shut the fuck up. No, I wasn't," I yell. In that instant, I regret yelling that loud. The band stops playing and stares at all five of us. I look around and notice more people have left, leaving the brewery prone to more people hearing us. Even the band.

"Keep playing. There is nothing going on here, just a couple of drunks," Cruz yells out to the band and they all nod in agreement and start the song back up again.

Just a couple of drunks? What the fuck? Cruz doesn't sound like he believes me.

"You need to leave," Cruz says to Chris.

"Not without her." Chris reaches for my arm. Cruz stops him before he reaches my arm and throws his arm back.

"Ashley, take Tessa to the back."

Ashley reaches out for my hand and I go with her, not looking back.

My head won't stop spinning. As we walk away, I bump into a chair, tripping over it, knocking it to the floor, and falling right on my hands and knees. The sound of the chair hitting the ground makes the band stop again, and everyone looks over at me.

"Goddamn it." I hear Cruz say in the background. I glance behind me and watch both Cruz and Chris come to my side, trying to help me up. "Are you okay?" Cruz asks.

I nod with tears coming down my face.

"Tessa! Get up. Let's go home," Chris yells out.

Ashley and Cruz are wide-eyed by the way he demanded me to go with him. I get up by myself and head for the back room with Ashley behind me. Before the door shuts, I hear Chris calling my name, and then the music plays again. My whole body is shaking at this point as I cry out loud. The stupid alcohol isn't helping the situation. I can't even hold myself together.

"Tessa, come sit down," Ashley mutters. I follow her and sit down in Cruz's office chair.

"You believe me, right? That I wasn't with Chris last night?"

She says nothing and looks away from me.

"Ashley!"

"Of course I believe you. But I told you to be upfront with all this to Cruz if you were going to continue seeing him. I told you

I didn't want to see him hurt. I don't want to see you hurt, either. But look at the position you put him in."

Before I can answer, I hear the office door opening. Cruz walks in, looking between Ashley and me. "Are you okay?"

I nod, staying quiet. I don't want to say the wrong thing while under the influence of alcohol.

"Let me take you home," he says.

I gaze up at him wide-eyed and confused because I thought he wanted me to go over tonight. I didn't think this would change his mind. We talked about this a little while ago and he said he trusts me as long as I'm honest with him.

"I'll talk to you later." Ashley gives me a quick hug and walks out the door.

CHAPTER THIRTY

Tessa

WE WERE silent the entire drive back to my place. Cruz's forehead furrowed and his jaw tensed. So I remained silent, hoping he would say something.

He parks his truck in front of my stairs, doesn't put it in park, and looks straight ahead. My heart is hammering in my chest. I'm at a loss for words.

We both sit here in silence for a few minutes before Cruz says, "I need to get back."

"Are you mad at me?" I watch as he squeezes his steering wheel with both hands. "Cruz."

"I'm upset," he retorts.

"At me?"

"At this whole situation."

"You don't believe him, do you?"

He stays silent, like he's thinking of the answer.

"No, I don't. But it doesn't make it any easier with how forthcoming you've been."

My eyes burn from the tears that are resurfacing. My entire face throbs from sobbing and the booze. "We just talked about this and you said you trusted me. You asked me to be honest with you and I'm being honest with you. I wasn't with him."

"Tessa! He came into my business. A business I built from the ground up. It's one thing that he came in, but it's another when everything started a scene. The band even stopped playing, for Christ's sake. That's embarrassing. This is a small town. Reputation means everything to businesses here. More than half our business is from tourists. And the tourists are the ones who leave the most reviews."

"It sounds like you are blaming me?" I mutter.

He puts the truck in park and rolls down his window. A soft breeze flows through the window toward my face. "I need to go."

"Can we talk tomorrow?"

"I need some time, Tessa."

My heart drops from those words and I'm about to be sick. I put my hand over my mouth and rush out of the truck up to my studio. I type in the passcode and rush to the bathroom and vomit everything out.

The birds chirping outside wake me up, although my body doesn't feel like I slept at all. It feels more like I fainted and I'm now waking up. I open my eyes and look around, confused about where I am. The chilly surface beneath my backside is causing me pain. I move my hands across the floor and realize I'm lying on my bathroom floor. As I peel myself up, the bathroom floor feels plastered to my back. My head pounds more, and the throbbing ache behind my eyes worsens. I raise myself to a standing position and look at myself in the mirror. My eyes are red and puffy. A crippling pain attacks my body even more as I walk over to my bed. I reach for my phone and see it's five in the morning. I don't remember when I got home or how much actual sleep I've gotten. Flashbacks from last night are flooding my brain. I'm not even sure what's real and what's not. I bring my legs up to my chest and make myself fall back asleep.

A vibration from my phone jolts me awake. I lean over and glance at it, seeing that June is calling me. It's now ten o'clock, and my shift began an hour ago. Before I find anything to wear, I jump out of bed and go to the bathroom to brush my teeth.

I'm running down to the shop, tying my hair up in a bun and trying not to vomit from all the quick movements I've done in the last ten minutes. As I enter the backroom, I come to a halt to collect my breathing and force the vomit down. Oh God, I shouldn't have come today. My head pounds behind my eyes, making it harder to move around. I carefully walk up to the front and place my arm against my brows to shield the sunlight as I take a peek around and see if there are any customers.

"Where have you been?"

I'm startled by the sound of June's voice. "I'm sorry I overslept." I turn around and face her.

Her eyes go wide, shaking her head. She grabs me by the arm and pulls me to the back with her. "You need to go."

"What? Why?"

"You look terrible."

"I had a rough night. I'll be fine." While holding my mouth closed, I turn away from her. Shit, I'm not fine. I'm going to be sick.

"I know a hungover person when I see one. This establishment will not be known for hungover workers."

Great, I'm no longer wanted at Cruz's brewery or June's

store in less than twenty-four hours. I return upstairs to do my business in the restroom. A warm bowl of chicken noodle soup sounds satisfying. It's my go-to hangover remedy. It's always made me feel better. I sit down and drink little sips of the juice while soaking saltine crackers in it. The small bit of soup I could eat made me much more fatigued than I was before. I go up, close the blinds on all my windows, and lie down again. As I put my phone on silent, I see no one has contacted me. Even though I hadn't high expectations of Cruz getting in touch with me, I did with Ashley and she hasn't contacted me either. As I set my phone down, I crawl deeper into my covers to fall back asleep.

I'm awakened by small knocks coming from my door. I slowly stand up and walk toward the window, double-checking that it isn't Chris. Ashley stands there with a brown bag in her hand. Before opening the door, I stop and think for a second, wondering if it's my stuff I've left at Cruz's house.

"Hey," Ashley says quietly, with a sympathetic tone. I take a few steps back, giving her room to walk in. "I brought my favorite hangover food." She lifts the bag up. My stomach growls. It's been a day since I ate last except for the small sips of the soup I had earlier.

"What time is it?" I ask.

"Almost five."

"Five. Holy shit, I've been asleep all day."

"Have you?" she asks and starts pulling the food out of the bag.

I take a seat and look at everything she ordered. "Sushi is your hangover food?"

"Yup and Pad Thai."

Interesting combination. She opens a huge order of Pad Thai and places it between us. I reach over and open the big round container that holds four sushi rolls. "You ordered a lot of food?"

She hands me chopsticks. "I wasn't sure how hungry you

would be. I'm usually starving for carbs after I indulge myself with a lot of alcohol the night before."

We both stay silent as we eat. I keep waiting for her to bring up last night, but she doesn't. I'm sure she's hoping I will bring it up so she can see if I'm open to discussing it or not. I'm not sure what to ask or say. Sometimes I feel as though what I'm thinking didn't happen. I watch us both eat simultaneously. Each of us not making much eye contact with one another.

I clear my voice. "So how is he? Is he really upset?"

She looks up at me mid-bite and sets her chopsticks down. "And hurt."

"Should I leave him alone?"

She gives me a side-eye. "I don't know what to tell you. I've never seen him fall for someone like he has fallen for you. I told you from the start he likes honesty. I also told you I didn't want to see him get hurt. He's family to me."

"Will he be mad at you that you came over here?" I wait for her to finish chewing before she answers.

She wipes her mouth with a napkin. "He doesn't know. But he's not like that either. He likes open, honest communication. I'll obviously tell him I came to see you. He will not get mad, nor will he push to know what we talked about. He gives his trust to people easily. Because he believes everyone deserves the benefit of the doubt before they don't. He's heard about you and your ex, but he trusted you to be upfront about it. But you never were, and more and more stuff kept going around that he kept hearing."

I set my chopsticks down and lay my head on one of my hands. This is all too much in such a short amount of time. It's hard to not want to give up. I tried to start a new life. I prayed this wouldn't happen, and it did. "We talked about it before last night and he said he trusted me and wanted me to be honest with him. I'm being honest."

"You have to understand last night could've hurt his business. He doesn't mess around when it comes to his business."

"I know."

"Give him some time and then go talk to him."

I wipe a tear that falls down my face. "Thank you for coming over. I thought I had no one after last night."

The look on Cruz's face last night still worries me. I've never seen him this mad. I would rather clear things up with him sooner rather than later. He did say to give him some time. Ashley said the same thing. I better listen to Ashley and give him some space before I make things even worse.

CHAPTER THIRTY-ONE

IT'S BEEN a week since that disastrous night and a week since I've spoken with Cruz. I followed Ashley's advice and I'm giving him space. I'm not sure how much time I should give him, and he hasn't contacted me either. This week I've been keeping to myself. I've done nothing but sleep, work, and mope around my studio. I haven't even seen Ashley. She made it clear that she wasn't upset with me. Cruz has been her best friend for quite some time. She has more loyalty to him than to me. I get it, that's why I haven't pushed either.

Chris is still acting erratically. He appears and disappears. I haven't spoken to him, but when I'm at home, I hear him knocking on my door and yelling my name. I don't answer. Instead, I sit in silence and wait for him to leave. I'm surprised he hasn't called, but I'm sure he doesn't have a phone since he doesn't have a job. I thought about following him once after he left my house one night to see where he goes. But I decided against that because I don't want to be associated with him in any way. I'm also shocked he hasn't gone inside to look for me. At times, I have the impression that someone is controlling him, but I'm not sure who it would be. How can someone be this strange and appear out of nowhere? It's almost as if he comes by every now and then to see how I'm doing. Or to make sure I'm still around. Everything he says to me about getting an apartment for us is probably a front. A front for him to continue showing up. I don't know anyone who would be interested enough in what I'm doing to ask him to keep an eye on me. However, it still makes little sense. I know he's using, but I doubt he'd be this erratic.

I've thought about leaving and starting over. But then thoughts of Cruz run through my head and all the memories we've made in such a short period stop me. And I don't want to leave. I'm becoming more accustomed to this small town now. I like how everything is in walking distance. It's nice to walk a few blocks for groceries or a meal. Driving to nearby places takes longer. It's a small town, but it almost feels like I'm a city person. Like how most of the people who live in the city walk everywhere to get to places. In small towns, walking to a place may only be half a mile, unlike big cities where it can take miles.

Today I took myself out to get some fresh air. I came to the Arches National Park that everyone talks about. The Delicate Arch Trail is 3.2 miles long round trip. I haven't been too active since being here. I'm a little worried about my health with all the social drinking I've been doing. As I hike up the trail, I keep seeing families and couples hiking the trail together. It makes me a little sad, wishing I were experiencing this with someone. When I Googled about the trail, it said to go when the sun is setting because you can catch a beautiful sunset. The trail isn't too bad. It feels like the whole thing is paved, but it's the rock. With the sun setting, the air is a lot cooler, and it feels good.

I finally get to the top and notice the arch. It's larger than I imagined. Due to the crowd, I decided not to go directly under the arch. I take a moment to rest before moving down. There is also a large spherical bowl-shaped opening. You could walk around. It seems like walking the entire circle could take a mile. The sunset colors shine through the arch as I look up. It makes it more appealing. Almost looks like it's a painting.

"Excuse me."

A lady approaches me from my left with a phone in hand.

"Do you mind taking a picture of my husband and me?"

"Sure." I stand up and reach out for her phone. "Do you guys want the arch and sunset in the background?" They both nod. I put the phone up and angle it the best I can. The husband wraps his arm around her. I take multiple photos so they can decide which ones they like the best. As I'm about to stop, the husband leans in to kiss her on her forehead. "Wait, do that again." He leans back in and I take as many as I can.

The lady walks back over to me. I hand her back her phone. She stands there scrolling through all the pictures. "Thank you. These are great."

I give her a smile.

"Are you here by yourself?" she asks.

"Yeah."

"Do you want me to take some pictures of you with the sunset and arch?"

"Umm. Sure." We switch places as I hand her my phone. Doing this alone makes me feel awkward. I'm not sure how to stand or pose. I do the best I can.

She walks back over to me. I reach for the phone and scroll through the pictures. *Okay, they're not so bad.* "Thank you. Are you guys here visiting?"

"Yes. My husband loves to travel to all the national parks. I'd rather be lying out on a beach, but we compromise the best we can." She chuckles. I watch as her husband walks up behind her and places his hand on her lower back. Watching them makes me miss Cruz even more. The nice, gentle touches from him made me feel so safe. "Are you visiting?"

"No. I actually moved here a few months ago."

"Oh nice. What made you come here?"

"I randomly picked a place I thought would be nice to start over at."

"Oh yeah, we've done that a few times. Everywhere we visit, we want to move there. So we did a few times. It sometimes gets expensive and tiring. We're trying to be absolutely sure of the next place we move to. It's been fun learning different cultures of each place we've lived at."

"That would be so fun to get to live in different places. I'm Tessa, by the way." I reach out to shake her hand.

"I'm Kenzie and this is my husband, Mike."

"Nice to meet you, guys. It was nice talking to you. I'm going to head back down before it gets darker."

"We should do that too," she says, turning to her husband.

"Do you know any good places here to eat?" Mike asks.

"Cruz Brewery Co. is great. You guys should try it." I watch as Mike searches for it on his phone.

"Nice. It's close to where we are staying. Thanks."

"Anytime," I say and head back.

Hopefully recommending Cruz's brewery will help with what I wrecked.

CHAPTER THIRTY-TWO

Tessa

"WHAT'S HAPPENING with you lately? The past couple of weeks you've been moping around," June asks.

"Nothing." I hang some of the new clothes we got in. All items in the shipment are from the 1920s. A ton of flapper dresses, white sleeves, and pearl necklaces came in. I don't understand where they come from. It's pretty cool that someone saved these after all these years.

"Here." June hands me more dresses to hang up. I throw them over my shoulder as I hang each one up. "I may be old, but I'm not senile. I can tell when something is off."

It's been another week, and I still haven't heard from Cruz. Each day that passes makes me worried even more that he's done with me. I'm confused about how that night at his brewery has caused him to be this angry. I have a gut feeling there is something else going on, but I'm not sure what it is. This week has been an emotional rollercoaster for me. I'm annoyed that he hasn't spoken to me. But then I realize I can't be upset because I haven't reached out to him. Sometimes I feel lost and don't know what to do. I'm not sure what he wants. This is all new to me and I was trying to give him his space like he asked.

Ashley and I had dinner once this past week. I didn't ask why we haven't talked much lately. I don't want to get between her and Cruz. She told me Cruz was doing okay. He's keeping busy with work. She knows he misses me. But he's back to being uptight.

I swallow the lump in my throat. "I'm having relationship problems."

"With that boy Cruz?"

I nod.

"This is why I never got married. Men are boys in a grown-up body. They never mature. Why do you think I have lived for so long?"

I burst out laughing. "I thought it was because you never had kids?"

"Well, that too. Kids suck the life out of you."

"Didn't you ever get lonely?"

"Nah. I had a lot of friends. And their kids were nice to be around. But never was what I wanted. I could do whatever I wanted. Leave whenever I wanted. I didn't have to worry about no one. It keeps your stress down. I swear that's why I'm still alive and my friends aren't."

I'm always surprised by how well she does here, especially with the boxes we get shipped to us. June's words hold some truth.

"What's the problem with you and that boy?" she says with a sidelong glance.

"To tell you the truth, I don't even know. We got into an argument a couple weeks ago and we still haven't talked." If you call that an argument. I don't know what it was. A disagreement?

"And you're still going to waste your time on him?"

My eyes go wide as I turn to look at her. "Are you sure you really didn't like being in a relationship, or did you give no one a chance?"

"Don't get smart with me," she mutters.

I giggle a little. "That's what it sounds like. So you think I should be done with Cruz because of one argument?"

"Honey, I think you two are already done if you both have let two weeks pass by without speaking to each other."

"Then what would you have done?" I turn to her after putting the last of the dresses up. I grab the box and start breaking it down to throw away.

"If I hadn't heard from him in over twenty-four hours, I would have marched right up to him, told him to stop beating around the bush and talk this out." She crosses her arms and nods like she's lecturing me.

I can't help but smile because of how funny she is when I know she's trying to be serious. She's right. Why am I waiting around for him to talk to me? Two weeks is plenty of time to give someone. "Thanks, June. I'm going to go talk to him." I head toward the backroom to throw the box away.

"Not until after your shift is over, missy." I hear her say in the distance.

"Of course, June," I yell.

I twirl and examine myself in the mirror before heading over to the brewery. Hopefully, Cruz is there. It's been two miserable weeks since I've been there. I'm actually missing the brewery, too. To make sure he couldn't resist me, I threw on a white summer dress with straps that form a halter top around my neck and reveal my back. It's a V-cut, so it shows off my boobs just enough without looking like I'm trying too hard. I put on a full face of makeup and curled my hair. Maybe I went too far, but I'm not sure where he stands with us right now. I want him to want me. My nude sandals are the right pop of color. Not too subtle, but not too bold.

The closer I get to the brewery, the more my nerves shake through my body. I had to run positive scenarios through my head to keep me from turning back around. When he sees me, I want him to run up to me and wrap me in his arms, kiss me and tell me how much he's missed me. A girl can dream. Once I reach the door, I stop and inhale a huge breath. I'm feeling light-headed. I don't know if it is from my nerves working my body up or because I was holding my breath in. I distance myself from the door and brush my hand over my forehead.

"Are you okay, miss?" a guy trying to get inside asks.

"Um. Yes, I'm fine. Thank you."

"You should sit down."

"I will. I need a minute." He stands there for a few more seconds and then heads inside.

I take a couple more deep breaths before swinging open the door and walking in. Tonight isn't as crowded as it usually gets, making it easy to find him if he is here. He could be in the back. I also don't see Ashley. It could be her day off? I move a few steps forward, past the hostess stand, and take a glance around. A flirty laugh attracts my attention to my left. I noticed a woman and a man in a booth, with her sitting in front of him. As I'm turning to look in the opposite direction, I stop myself. I tilt my head back that way. Something didn't look right over there.

My pupils dilate, and my heart sinks to my gut. What the fuck is going on? The man in front of this woman is Cruz. He looks deep in thought. She's giggling and twirling her hair around her fingers as if she's trying to win him over with her cutesy gestures.

Cruz must notice someone has been standing here close to

the hostess stand because his eyes gaze over at me. I glare between him and the woman, who is now directing her attention at me and him. I back up a few steps, shaking my head. How is this possible? How could he move on so quickly? I expected him to get out of the booth, come to me and say, "This isn't what it looks like." But he doesn't. He turns back around, faces the woman, and continues their conversation. She sits there smiling at him and continuing to twirl her hair between her fingers.

I swiftly turn around and return home. This must be how it feels to have your heart ripped out of you. This chest pain I'm feeling caught me off guard. Chris made me feel heartbroken, but Cruz's actions have caused me even more pain.

I rip my clothes off the second I get home and wash all my makeup off. What's left of it after crying. I crumple onto my bed and huddle into a ball. This is unbelievable. I never expected this from him. Is it possible that I misread him? He never appeared to be a player, and no one ever spoke about him in that way. Why do I constantly have bad luck in my life? This irritates me. First, it was my mother, then Chris, and now Cruz. Why can't I live a regular life? All I want is a normal life with someone. Someone to return home to after a long day of work. Have dinner together, unwind, and wake up next to each other every morning.

I debate texting Ashley to see if she knows anything. But stop myself. I can't always run to her. This is too much for me.

I hear a knock on the door and hold my breath, as if they can hear me.

"Tessa. It's me." My heart sinks even lower than I could ever imagine it doing. Cruz is outside my door. "It's not what you think." And there are the words every man who gets caught says. I sit up, deciding if I should open the door or not. I can't get myself to move more than this. Little knocks are still coming from the door. "Tessa. She's an investor. She wants to invest in my brewery and open up another one in Colorado." I say nothing back and neither does he.

I continue to sit here silently until I hear him walk down the steps. His footsteps become more distant by the minute. I want to run out there, hug him, and kiss him. But I also want to run out there and yell at him. I'm so confused and hurt. Knowing I deserve more than what this life has handed me stops me.

CHAPTER THIRTY-THREE

HERE I AM, back to square one. Hurt, lost, and confused like I was before I moved here. I trusted another guy not to hurt me. When will I ever learn? It's been a few days since I walked into the brewery and saw what I saw. Cruz keeps texting me, trying to reassure me it's not what it looked like. He hasn't stopped by here either. I'm assuming he's respecting my space until I'm ready. It's a circle that never ends.

Why does he care now after I saw him with her? He never attempted to talk to me during those two weeks. It makes little sense.

The creaks to the door echo throughout the store as someone walks in. I come around the shelves to greet that person. It's Ashley standing there, looking over at me. She walks up and pulls me into a hug.

"Hey. How have you been?"

I shrug my shoulders as my response because I still don't even know.

"It's been a rough month for you and Cruz."

My brow furrows when I realize it's been three weeks since Cruz and I last spoke. Everything happened so quickly that I didn't realize how much time had passed. When you're miserable and lonely, time moves slowly.

"When are you off work?"

"We're closing up in an hour." I walk back over to the counter.

Ashley follows me. "How about I come over later with dinner?"

"You don't have to do that. You're always trying to cheer me up and check up on me. I'm probably a burden on you now."

"Shut the fuck up. You're not a burden to me. This bullshit that you and Cruz have going on is hurting me, too. I hardly see you anymore. Cruz is on edge now. I have to walk on eggshells around him to make sure I don't say the wrong thing. Trust me. Right now, he's more of a burden than you."

I chuckle a little, relieved to hear that I'm not the only one being affected by all this. It sounds bad, but it feels good that he's also hurting.

"Close up and I'll meet you back here." She walks out the door. The fucking creaks ring through my ears again. I never realized how much I hated those creaks until now. I used to like them because it would let me know if someone was here, but now they can fuck off.

I burst out laughing. "What do you mean, he's being a big baby?"

"He's crying about everything now. Girl, you two need to get your shit straightened out, or all of us at the brewery are going to have heart attacks. And then he will really have something to cry about. Because all his employees will be dead and he'll have to pay out everyone's life insurance. The brewery will be forced to close because he'll end up broke and unable to pay anyone."

Ashley came over and brought us Chinese food from a local hole in the wall that I never knew existed until now. Once again, she ordered way too much. She likes to order different foods on the menu so she can enjoy a variety. I don't get why she keeps doing that because she's eaten at every place here. She should know what she likes.

"If he's been hurting so bad, why hasn't he talked to me?" I ask.

"Well, why haven't you talked to him?"

"Because he told me to give him time. So I respected that. I thought he would come to me when he was ready to talk. But that didn't happen. And then I find him, with that bimbo eye fucking him."

"You two are both hard-headed. Trust me, he was waiting around for you, too."

"Why didn't you tell me?"

"You two are grown adults. You guys should be able to figure this out on your own." She walks over to my bed and lies down.

I pick up all the food and place the leftovers in the fridge. "You talk about us like we're children who don't know how to make decisions." Ashley's head lifts a little off the bed with her brows raised as I glance over at her. "Shut up." I caught on to what I just said. We really haven't been able to make decisions. "So then it's true? That bimbo he was with was an investor?"

"Yes. But I don't think he's going to move forward with her."

I get the rest of the food in the fridge and lie next to Ashley. I'm kind of glad to hear those words. From the way she was acting, it seemed like all she wanted to do was get into his pants. "Why do you say that?"

"He enjoys keeping the brewery here and only here. He likes the small-town feel of everything and if his brewery grows, he doesn't feel like it will still feel that way. Who knows, maybe one day he'll want to go big. But for now, he likes what he has."

Ashley and I keep talking about many different topics. She told me even more about her and Cruz's childhood. It made me happy that they could grow up this way. Back then, it was an even smaller town. Every night after school, they would play night games. When the streetlights turned on, they knew it was time to go home. Every weekend was a new adventure. Swimming in the river, going hiking, or biking. When they were teenagers, they would take their trucks out to the desert, drop the tailgates, and party all weekend. They'd have kegs after kegs and massive bonfires for light. They wouldn't leave until the bonfire was done burning, and that was usually when the sun was coming up.

"I wish my childhood had been like that." Instead of coming home from school wondering what was going to happen next, my life has always been on edge. I had a great life after I moved in with my grandparents, but I was still always on edge. Wondering when my mom was coming home. How she was going to look. Would she be clean? Sometimes, I dreamed about a happy family. I would come home from school and my mom would be home waiting for me. We would start on homework together until it was time for her to cook dinner. I would help her cook until Dad got home and we would all sit around the dining room table and eat, talk, and laugh together. My dad would help clean up the kitchen while I went to my room and played. And then at the end of the night, my parents would tuck me in, kiss me on the cheek, and read me a goodnight story. Maybe that's why I want that life. The life living in a house with a white picket fence, waving my husband off to work while I attend to the kids. Because I had nothing close to that growing up. I've worked so hard to have the life that I'm living. I will not give up on it now.

"You should have moved down here sooner. We would have had tons of fun." A yawn comes from Ashley, making me yawn.

We're both lying side by side on my bed. It's been refreshing to have someone by my side. I'm always here alone and sometimes hate it. Because I overthink. Overthinking causes me so much stress and worry. It's nice to have a night free of that. "You don't think we have fun now?" I ask.

"We do, but it's different when you have responsibilities."

It is different. But I have more fun now than I did in my childhood. "Do you ever see much of your family?" I say as I turn over to my side to face Ashley. Her eyes are closed and her breathing has evened out. She's fast asleep.

I turn to my phone and notice it's three o'clock in the morning. I didn't realize it was this late. Time went by fast. I'm not as tired as I usually am. Thinking about the future has my brain running. After tonight, I feel much more comfortable talking everything out with Cruz. It's hard starting a new relationship. You're still learning the ins and outs of each other and their wants and needs. I've never had much luck with relationships, and Cruz was always too busy with creating his life to take dating seriously. We both need to sit down and talk and clear the air about everything. Whether or not we want to both move forward together. Something needs to be decided. We can't keep living in limbo.

CHAPTER THIRTY-FOUR

Tessa

"WHAT ADDRESS WOULD you like this shipped to?" I ask the customer I've been helping for what seems like years. She came in looking for a wooden chest for a pirate theme she is planning on doing to her bar. A bar that she and her husband built in their home. I can hardly pay attention. My mind has been on Cruz this whole day. After work, I want to go over to this house and talk to him. Ashley told me he isn't working tonight, so I figured tonight would be the best time to talk. If he's home.

"Make sure you package this so it doesn't get damaged," the lady says.

"I will," I say with a slight smile. I'm trying hard not to give her any attitude. But I'm sick of talking to her. She has gone on and on about every little thing that she's been doing to her house, giving me her entire life story. I know she means well. I'm just not in the mood for it.

"And if it's not packaged correctly, and it gets damaged, I will be requesting a full refund."

"Okay." Is all I can say. After another twenty minutes of her rambling on about something, I finally get her out the door. With a heavy sigh, I walk back over to June, who is watching me from the counter. I raise my eyes toward her, at a loss for words. I'm so worn out and all I keep running through my mind is what I'm going to say to Cruz. Which I've come up with nothing.

"What's your deal today?" June asks as I walk toward the back and take a seat. She follows me and sits across from me.

"Nothing." I let my head fall back.

"You haven't talked to Cruz yet, have you?"

"No. But I'm going to after work."

"I thought you said last week you were going to talk to him?"

I rise and begin closing the store to keep my mind busy. "I went, but something came up and I never got the chance to speak to him." I don't tell her about the investor. She already thinks we are both wasting our time. I don't wait to hear what she has to say and I walk out to the front to clean up. Right now, I don't want any more opinions until he and I sort this out.

I've finally finished getting ready. I put on another pretty summer dress. This one is cream in tone and covered in flowers. After applying a little makeup, I pulled my hair into a high ponytail. I take another glance in the mirror, call it good, and leave. As soon as I step outside, there's something crunchy under my foot. From the top of the steps to the bottom, I see red rose petals everywhere. What the hell? Who did this? No one is in sight. But then my heart sinks a little. What exactly is Cruz up to? As I walk down, I slow my steps and look around to see if I can find him or his truck, but neither is around. When I reach the bottom of the stairs, I hear faint footsteps approaching. When I turn toward the footsteps, I see who's approaching me. All I want to do is scream and cry.

Chris is now standing in front of me with his body twitching as he drops to one knee. "I told you I wanted to marry you and I'm making you that promise." He reaches up for my hand, but I pull it away before he can grab it.

"What are you doing? Get up!" I yell as I hold my hands away from him.

"I know things haven't been easy between us and this time apart has made me realize I love you with everything I have."

"Shut up. You have nothing. You don't even have me. Why do you keep showing up out of nowhere? I haven't seen you in weeks and here you are acting like a damn idiot." I take a few steps and hear a car coming closer toward us. Great, this is going to be embarrassing whoever sees us. One more thing I'll have to explain to Cruz. The closer the sound gets, the more familiar it sounds. I look over and see headlights shining at us. The second the truck stops, my heart sinks. Cruz gets out of the truck, rage on his face, and stares at what's in front of him.

"Cruz. It's not what it looks like." Is all I can say. I realize those are the words I told myself that every guy says when they're caught and guilty of something. Chris stands up and walks over to Cruz. I grab his hand to stop him. He throws his hand out of mine.

"What's your problem, man? Can't you see she doesn't want you?" Chris says.

"What the fuck! No! I don't want you," I say, looking at Chris. I turn to Cruz and notice he has a bouquet of pink and white lilies in his hand. As I gaze at Cruz's face, I swallow the lump in my throat. His shoulders are slumped over, and so is his face. He looks as if there is nothing more between us. His silence is even more terrifying. He's giving up. "Cruz! It really isn't what it looks like."

"And what does it look like?" he asks.

"It looks like we're getting married," Chris says and then jumps at the sound of a twig breaking in the distance.

Both Cruz and I stare at him, wondering what's so startling about that sound. But that's the way he is from using.

"I was going over to your house to talk to you and I walked out to this," I say, pointing at the stairs that lead to my studio. "I didn't ask for this. You told me to be honest with you and I am. I don't want him. I told you how he is and this is another erratic thing he is doing. Trust me, Cruz," I say as tears well up in my eyes.

Chris pushes me aside and steps in front of me. I keep myself from falling to the ground and watch as Cruz moves closer to Chris. He raises his fist and slams a punch right into his right cheek, knocking him down to the ground. I'm glancing between Cruz and Chris, dumbfounded by what he's done. Chris lies senseless on the ground, moaning in pain and covering his face with his hands.

"Don't fucking touch her," Cruz yells and then looks over at me. His face is flushed and his jaw is clenched. "I'm too old for this, Tessa. This is some childish shit."

"Why do you keep blaming me for his actions? Don't you think I know this is childish? He's a drug addict who can't get a grip on me not wanting to be with him and I've moved on."

The combination of whatever Chris is on and Cruz's fist is making Chris look more in a daze than he was before. Does he have a concussion now? We watch as he slowly stands up, looking between the two of us as if he's confused about why he is here. He stumbles back from us and walks away.

"You think I want this pathetic loser?" I say, pointing to Chris. "I was coming to talk to you. This is ridiculous what we've been doing here, Cruz."

"What have we been doing?" He crosses his arms and gives me a glare.

"This!" I wave my hands between both of us. "It's been almost a month since we've talked. You say this is childish. Not talking is childish."

"I don't think this is going to work."

My heart stops beating the moment those words leave his mouth. His demeanor changed, as if there is nothing left between us. The bouquet has been stomped flat to the ground by his feet. I return my gaze to him and notice the pain in his eyes. My thoughts are all over the place. I can't seem to think straight. I'm so confused by what's going on. We discussed it over dinner, and he told me he trusts me and to be honest with him. Which I have been. What has changed since our conversation? My tears have finally dried up from the uncertainty of it all.

"What are you thinking?" he mumbles.

"Are you serious? That is the question you're going to ask me?" Now I'm getting heated.

Cruz takes a few steps closer to me as I take a few steps back, bumping my back into the stairs railing. "Please, give it some time," he says.

I look at him, baffled. "Give it some time! Don't you think I have been giving it some time? I gave it some time when all that shit went down at the brewery. I gave it time when I found that bimbo trying to jump into your pants. I have been giving it time. So what time are you talking about?" We both stand there in silence. The sun has now set all the way and the darkness from the sky is making it hard to read his facial expressions. The one light pole that is back here is barely giving us any light. "Do you have anything to say?" I ask.

"Some things are hard to explain right now."

"What! What does that even mean? Nothing is making sense, Cruz. What happened between the talk we had over dinner to now?"

"Tessa, please just give it some time," he mutters.

I throw my hands down to my sides and ball my fists. "Stop saying that if you will not give me an explanation. What time do you need?" He runs his hands through his hair and turns his back toward me. "Your silence speaks louder than words." And with that, I head back upstairs. I try my hardest not to look back at him. Once my door is shut and I lean my back against the wall, my chest shakes, and the tears flow.

CHAPTER THIRTY-FIVE

DESPITE MY DIFFICULT CHILDHOOD, I have never felt as alone as I do now. My life is such a mess. More than I thought it ever would be. It's been a couple of weeks since I last saw Cruz. I've been coming to terms with the fact that we tried and it didn't work out. If this is what he wants, then this is what I'll give him. I can't fight for someone who doesn't want me. In all honesty, I'm too tired to fight. Something has felt off for a while now and I've tried to talk to him about it, but he always said everything was fine. I can't force something that doesn't belong.

I've been keeping myself busy the best I can while avoiding the places I could run into Cruz at. I'm glad I at least know his work schedule, so when I have to go out somewhere, I know I have a chance to not run into him.

"Are you sure you don't want me to help you with anything?" I ask. June invited me over for dinner. When she asked me, my mouth fell open in shock.

I have a strong sense that June knows more than she lets on. She has asked nothing since that day Cruz ended things for good. I still wonder if there is a camera outside, and she watched everything play out. If she does, she hides it well because I can't find it. Usually, she would question my sadness. But lately she hasn't. I've tried my best not to let it affect my work since June doesn't like our personal lives to affect work. I can only avoid so much sadness. Sometimes I have good days and think I'm getting over this hard hump in my life. Then the sadness shocks me out of nowhere.

"No, just sit there," she says.

I laugh at how bossy she can be. I observe her sauteing onion and garlic in olive oil for the spaghetti sauce. Her house reminds me of the 1970s, with orange carpet, dark wood everywhere, and a white popcorn ceiling. I was stunned to see all her old appliances still in use. The refrigerator is a yellow mustard color. It almost appears to have been white before turning into that color. The oven is also green. My guess is that homeowners did not match the colors of their appliances like they do now.

"How long have you lived here?" I take a sip of the cabernet she poured for us.

"A long time. Since the '70s." She throws garlic bread into the oven.

"Have you always lived alone?"

"Yes. I told you. I've never been married." She comes and sits by me with her wine glass in her hand. "The food should be done soon."

I nod. "You've never lived with any friends?"

"Nah. They all got married and had kids. Back then, everyone would marry young and start a family. Not me, though," she says with a chuckle.

I want to ask her if she knows anything about Brayden. Like where he came from? Something seems off about him since he returned to town. I'm trying not to rely on the fact that he may be the one who caused this to happen between Cruz and me. But that gut feeling keeps nudging at me.

The oven timer goes off and I watch as June gets up to pull the bread out of the oven.

"Can you set the table?"

I nod and head over to the kitchen.

"Silverware is in there." She points to a drawer next to the sink. "And place mats are in the drawer underneath it."

I'm not sure if we'll need a fork, spoon, or knife, but I take them all, regardless. I walk over to the kitchen table, grab a couple of napkins from the napkin dispenser, and place the silverware on top of the napkins. I return to the kitchen to get the place mats and bring them to the table. After the table is all set, I see June adding the spaghetti into fancy serving bowls to set on the table.

"Are these ready to take to the table?" I ask.

"Yes. Grab some more place mats to set them on."

I do what she asks and start setting out the dinner on the table. June sets our plates on our place mats as I take a seat.

"Serve yourself," she says.

Not much was spoken during dinner and I was having a hard time trying to bring up Brayden. I wonder if June thought I needed the company regardless if we talked or not. Once you get to know her, she has such a big heart without trying to show it too much. This is one occasion she shows how big it can truly be.

After we cleaned up dinner, June asked if I wanted a bowl of ice cream. We're now out on her back porch, watching the sun go down. "Is this a nightly routine of yours?"

"This?" she says and lifts her bowl.

"Yeah. Do you come out here every night and watch the sunset?" I'm trying hard to ease into another conversation.

"Most nights."

"We have something in common." I chuckle. "I do this a lot, too."

She turns her head toward me. "Where do you sit? In the parking lot?"

"No. The small little space I have between the stairs and my front door is enough space for one chair." I shrug my shoulders. "It works." Her expressions don't seem too amused with our similarities. Asking her about anything isn't going to work tonight. The conversations feel forced at this point. "Well, June, it's getting late. I'm going to head out." She looks down at her watch and then back up at me as I stand up.

"You don't have to go so soon."

"I walked over here and I'd rather get home before it gets darker outside."

She stands up and looks at her watch again. I furrow my brows while staring at her, wondering why she's so hesitant for me to leave. Maybe she's the one who needed company tonight and asked me over. She has mentioned a lot of her friends have passed away. I grab her bowl from her hands and head back inside to wash them. She follows behind me.

"Thank you for inviting me over for dinner. It was delicious. I miss home-cooked meals."

She nods and starts drying the dishes. "You don't cook for yourself?"

"I haven't lately. I used to cook a lot more."

After saying goodbye to June, I try to hurry and get to my place faster than normal. I'm usually not so timid, but right now, after everything, I'm kind of on edge walking home in the dark. The sun is barely visible. As I approach the parking lot, I abruptly stop. A dark figure is hunched over my car, looking into the passenger window. My breathing becomes shallow. Beads of sweat are dripping down my forehead. I glance around for anyone nearby. But there's no one. The guy looks like he's trying hard to see what I have in my car without shining a light into it. If he's trying to break in and steal something, I have nothing to steal. He's wasting his time. My heartbeat races as he stands up straight and turns around.

"Brayden!" I exclaim. He jumps at the sound of my voice. Or did he jump from being caught snooping in my car? "What are you doing?"

He brings one of his hands up and runs it through his hair. "Uh… I was checking to see if June left her keys in her car. She wanted me to look at something."

"But this is my car. June is at home. I just got back from her place."

He turns back around, stares at the car, and laughs. "My bad. I thought she left her car here for me to look at it." He steps closer to me and I back up a little. He notices my hesitation because he puts his hands up. "I'm sorry, Tessa. I didn't mean to scare you."

If June asked him to check out her car, how could he not know what it looks like? My thoughts on this town are changing by the minute. Nothing is making sense. Ashley said people move here to escape. It's making me think everyone here has a secret you have to watch out for. I swallow the lump in my throat. "It's okay. Simple mistake."

He crosses over both of his arms and stares at me as if I have more to stay. "How have you been?"

I do not want to start a conversation with him. Since he arrived, things have been off. My gut tells me there is more to him than I know. "As good as I can be. Cruz ended things with me."

His mouth drops as if he has sympathy for me. "I heard. I'm sorry."

A small chill runs through my body as we both stand in awkward silence, looking at one another. I'm getting the feeling June only asked me over for dinner so Brayden could snoop around. But what is he after? There is nothing here. It makes me a little sad that June now seems to be a part of this. I don't even know what this is.

"Give it some time. Things will work out."

My brows furrow. Those are the same words Cruz kept saying to me. I don't feel like I can trust anyone around here anymore. "You have a good night, Brayden," I say, trying to end the conversation. As I take a few steps back and begin walking up the stairs, I turn my head and see Brayden still standing there, watching me.

"Good night, Tessa." I shut myself inside my studio as chills run down my arms after hearing him say that in the distance.

CHAPTER THIRTY-SIX

Cruz

THIS PAINFUL AGONY I've been feeling is new to me. Even when my father died, I never felt this much pain. The hurt in Tessa's eyes when I told her it's done keeps replaying in my head. When I lie down after a long day, those eyes flash into my thoughts, keeping me awake all night. I haven't had a good night's rest since. The love I have for her is something I've never felt before. Something I never thought I would have. I didn't design my life to be trampled on by some newcomer to town. That's why I kept my distance from people. Tessa was different. In the end, she was the one I thought I would marry. I saw the hurt in her eyes the first night I laid eyes on her. Hurt I'm familiar with.

She came into the brewery alone, looking for something to eat. The eye contact we made every time I was closer to her showed the hurt. I saw the strength of her holding on. Something about her kept tugging me toward her. I wanted to know more about her while I comforted her from the pain she was holding onto. But she wouldn't open up to me. Everyone says I trust too easily, and maybe I do. I held on as long as I could, waiting for her to tell me something. Anything to make this all make sense. Day after day, nothing came. How can I blame her, though? I have my own *forbidden secrets* I keep locked away. *Forbidden secrets* no one will ever know.

It's been a month since I've seen or heard from her. Ashley knows not to bring her up. Ashley knows not to bring anything up. When Brayden told me everything, my world came crashing down. The one time I finally opened myself up to someone, now I'm questioning everything. Every night we spent together, every kiss, every touch. Was it all fake? I know people have a past, but is her so-called past really her past or is it her reality? I'm terrified of what's coming. And what will happen between Tessa and me when it arrives? As much as it pained me, I knew I had to let her go. I kept telling her to be patient. I expected everything to happen by now, but it hasn't. I just hope that after this is all said and done, she understands why I had to do it. Why I had to end something so special between us.

CHAPTER THIRTY-SEVEN

"COMING," I say as I hear a knock at my door. I swing open the door and see Chris standing at my doorway. He looks more nervous than I've ever seen before. What's he on now? His body trembles slightly with sporadic, bigger twitches. His eyes are bloodshot, with dark circles around his sunken eye sockets like he hasn't slept in days.

"You look like shit," I say. He rocks back and forth on his heels, looking behind me.

"Can we talk downstairs?"

"No. I have nothing to say to you. You ruined everything I built here. How much more do you need to take from me until you get the fucking point? I regret you. I always will."

"Tessa, please come down. There is something I want you to see."

"No!" I yell and take a few steps back and slam the door on

him. He puts his foot in the doorway, stopping it from shutting all the way.

"Tessa!" he says in a threatening voice. "If you don't come down, I will force my way in and make you come down."

"What the fuck do you want?" I continue slamming the door on his foot. He seems to not feel anything from it. His pain receptors are blocked by the drugs.

"Come on, Tessa. I don't want to hurt you."

"You already have!" I slam the door on his foot again. Hopefully, he feels some irritation from it to make him leave.

"Tessa."

I freeze at the sound of my name coming from the distance. No. No. No. This can't be. I haven't heard that voice since I was a child.

"Tessa. Please come here."

My heart rate speeds up, making my whole body shake from the sound of that voice. I slowly open the door. Chris moves over to the side and I see her standing there, dressed all in black with high heel boots on her feet. Her long brown hair flows with the small breeze. She's gained weight since the last time I've seen her. The color of her skin is pale white, but not in an unhealthy way. Her eyes aren't as sunken in as they used to be. She looks healthy.

I take a few more steps and look down. This can't be. I steady my pace and slowly walk down the stairs. "Mom." Her lips twitch in disgust at the sound of mom. We're face to face after my last step. Memories flood back of the pictures I stared at, wishing my mom would turn her life around and look like that again. And be the mother I wanted her to be. That seems like a century ago.

Chris has now come down the steps and the three of us are standing around in a small circle. I take a few steps back and look between her and Chris. "What is going on?"

"Your life looks like it turned out all right," my mom says.

My mouth drops. That's all she has to say to me. How long has she been clean? Why didn't she come back to me? After all these years, she's finally how I wanted my mother to be. Healthy and clean.

"Camile, let's just go. I told you I didn't want to do this."

"Shut the hell up, Chris. If you had followed through with what I paid you to do, we wouldn't be here."

I turn to Chris. "You know my mom?"

He says nothing. He doesn't even look at me.

"Oh, honey, don't you see? Chris was reporting back to me about your life. I wanted to see how your life turned out since you destroyed mine."

I shake my head. "What are you talking about?"

"I couldn't bear to see you happy."

"What! Isn't that what a mother would want for their child, to be happy?"

"No, why would I want that? Because of you, the only man I loved left me." My mom turns to Chris and slaps his hands. "Stop fidgeting. I told you to lay off that shit."

My brow furrows as I look between the two of them. There is some sort of relationship between them. Is she the reason Chris started doing drugs?

"Your dad couldn't handle you as a baby. It put a strain on our marriage and then he left."

"Then why did you two decide to have me? Why did you decide to start a family if you couldn't handle it?"

"We didn't think you would be such a hard baby to deal with. Your colic controlled our lives."

I raise my eyes in disbelief. "All because I had colic?"

"Yes. It was awful. We could never get you to stop crying. You kept us up all hours of the night. Sleep is very important and without proper sleep, you can't function as a human being. It makes you do things you wouldn't ever imagine doing. And then your dad left. It was too much for him to handle. He was falling behind at work. He couldn't pay the bills. After he left, I had to —well, you know. That's the only thing that numbed the pain."

Chris jumps back from the noise of a twig breaking. "Come on, we gotta get out of here," he says, looking around at our surroundings.

"I can't believe this," I say.

"I can't either, honey."

"Don't call me honey," I exclaim. "I can't believe you came from the people who had to raise me since you were a shitty mother. You're nothing like your parents. What happened to you? And what does Chris have to do with this?" I glance over at Chris and watch as he twitches to our surroundings. No one is near us. What is he nervous about?

"I paid him to make you fall in love with him and then leave you so you could feel the pain I felt when your dad left." She looks over at Chris and slaps him on the back of his head. "Except this idiot fell in love with you and wouldn't follow through with the plan. So I shot him up with a concoction I was experimenting with and, well, you know the rest."

Then realization hits me. He came home that night out of his mind, freaking out over something. He kept saying it was my fault. It was the drugs and my own mother.

"Get on the ground! Get on the fucking ground with your hands up!" multiple deep voices yell. When I glance at Mom, she raises her hands and widens her eyes. Men in black uniforms are swarming all around us. "Get on the fucking ground!"

Chris runs in the opposite direction but gets thrown down by the police with a stun gun. I slowly lower myself to the ground and raise my hands. There are about ten men in front of me with rifles aimed at us. My mother's expression says that there must be more of them in front of her. As I lie down on the ground, I watch as a bunch of men kneel on each of my mother's limbs and handcuff her.

"Tessa." Over all the commotion, I hear a softer voice above me. I'm too scared to move, so I stay lying down. A gentle touch grabs my hand. "Tessa, get up."

I raise my head and see Brayden in uniform, a rifle strapped behind his back. He helps me to my feet as I struggle to keep my balance. I'm in such a state of shock that I can't say anything. He wraps his arms around me and we walk to a black SUV. In the distance, I hear my mom yelling. I can't make out what she is saying. Brayden opens the car door for me and helps me in. My mom is being pushed into the car by the men as I watch. There is no sign of Chris anywhere. They must have him.

"Tessa, are you okay?"

I glance over my shoulder at Brayden and then back over at the chaos outside his car. My state of shock has me at a loss for words.

"I know it's a lot to handle right now. I hate to have to do this. I have to take you back to the station. We have some unanswered questions that we think only you can answer."

I stare outside as I watch them drive away with my mom in the back seat. "Am I under arrest?"

"No."

"Then how do you know I have the answers to your questions?"

Questions of my own need answers.

"Do you know the woman we arrested?"

I pivot my head and fixate on him with a lifeless gaze. "Yes."

"Then you have the answers that will help us."

I nod and we drive away from the chaos as he takes us to a place I never thought I'd step foot in.

CHAPTER THIRTY-EIGHT

I'VE BEEN SITTING HERE for what seems like an eternity. My body can't keep still. It doesn't help that this whole cement block room is so small. No wonder people fall under pressure. If this was the room where I was being interrogated, then I would fall, too. Oh wait, I am actually being questioned here.

I've been walking around in circles, trying to find answers to my own questions. Has my mom always been this unmotherly? I can't believe what she would do to her own flesh and blood. What made her turn out this way? The same people who raised her raised me. I turned out fine. She had a good childhood. Did the drugs change her?

I'm getting more nervous as time passes, even though they said I'm not arrested. I did nothing wrong. There is no reason to arrest me.

I hear the heavy door open and shut, shaking the two-way mirror I'm standing by. "Am I being set up? Am I going to jail? I didn't do anything!" I exclaim. The nerves running through my whole body make my voice shake.

"No, Tessa. I promise we really just have questions for you that we couldn't answer," Brayden says.

"Then why have I been sitting here like I'm a suspect? If they were simple questions, I would have been the first one you talked to." I lay my face down in my hands, trying to hold back the tears. I'm confused. None of this makes sense.

Brayden comes up and wraps his arms around me. My whole body shakes from the tears I held in. "I know this is all confusing. Sit down and we can talk." He leads me to the chair, sits me down, and hands me a bottle of water. I look at the water, wondering if he is trying to get my DNA or fingerprints. I've seen this play out many times on *SVU*.

My tears pour even harder. Brayden gives me a little time to cry. So we sit in silence. Before my sobs stop, the beating on the door startles me.

"Brayden!" Cruz yells.

I look up, wondering what he's doing here. We haven't spoken since that day he left me. Brayden cracks the door to speak. "Cruz, you can't be back here. Give us a minute."

"Is she in there?"

Brayden nods.

"Is she okay?"

"Yes. I promise. Wait outside and I'll bring her to you when I'm done."

"She needs me," he says in a soft voice.

"Yes, she does. So let us talk real quick."

Is Cruz part of this? I don't understand any of this. Why is he here? I thought he was done with me. None of this makes sense. Cruz must have walked away because I hear the door shut and Brayden takes his seat in front of me.

"Are you okay?" he asks.

"I need answers. Everything is spinning out of control. I don't understand any of this."

He nods. "Who is Camile to you?"

"My mother." Brayden's eyes go wide and he slumps a little further into his seat. My brows furrow. "Who is she to you guys?"

"She's the biggest drug mule in the western states. We've been trying to get her for years and she always gets away."

I howl in laughter hearing those words come out of his mouth.

He gives me a side-eye. "I'm glad you find this funny. I was worried about breaking the news to you once you said she was your mother."

"You gotta be kidding me, right? Her? A drug mule?" I lean my head back as more laughing escapes. "She couldn't even fend off a guy when I was growing up. How the hell did she pull that off?"

"I take it you two are not close?"

I wipe the tears from my eyes that have fallen from laughing. "Nope. I haven't seen her since I was twelve."

"Well, that explains the disconnect here. So your last name is Paige, and hers is Brown?"

"Yes. I took my grandparents' last name after they adopted me. Brown is my dad's last name. You guys didn't do your research very well."

"She has used so many aliases. We had a tough time finding her since it led us to other individuals who were not her. So why is she here now? You said you haven't seen her since you were twelve?"

"Apparently, she didn't want me to be happy, so she paid Chris to make me fall in love with him. Then leave me so I could be heartbroken like she was when my dad left her."

He gives me a questioning look. I explain everything I know

from my past until now. The more I tell him, the more worn out he's getting. He's slumped back in the seat with his arms crossed and one hand holding up his head, listening to me. As shocked as I am to find all this out and say it out loud to someone, it feels good to get all this off my chest. I wish it were Cruz I was confessing all this to. I have a feeling Brayden beat me to that. Well, at least what he knew.

I let out an enormous sigh after I finish telling him everything. He seems in disbelief because he sits there shaking his head.

"Wow. I'm sorry you went through all that."

"Now it's your turn. Tell me everything."

He sits up a little taller and lays both arms on the table. "What do you want to know?"

"I'm assuming you're not a travel agent for the wilderness?" I say with quotation marks in the air.

He chuckles. "No. I'm not. This is my job, taking the bad guys down."

My throat is so parched from crying, yelling, and talking. I finally get the courage to drink from the water bottle. I trust now that I'm not in trouble and they really needed to tie up loose ends. "So when we met at Sky Bar, who did you think I was?"

"I wasn't sure if you were involved. I'd been following Chris around for some time and he led me here. I caught the both of you outside talking a few times, so I followed you to the bar."

I give him a smirk. "Is this why you started talking to me?"

He nods. "I had to feel you out to see who you were."

"But you asked me out on a date?"

"Yes, to feel you out even more."

"That may be why you're still single, Brayden," I say sarcastically.

He laughs at my remark. "Yes, that is probably why."

"Was Cruz in on this? Are you and Cruz even friends?"

"Yes, we're friends. It wasn't until after I knew you two were dating that he found out."

My eyes grow wide in shock. "What! I didn't expect him to be involved."

"It's not what you think," he says while holding his hands up.

"Then start from the beginning," I say.

"Okay. You know I've been tracking Camile for a while now. When Chris came into the picture, you must have already left and come here because we knew nothing about you. We knew Camile was using Chris for her little games, but we didn't know what she was up to yet. When we followed Chris over here, we couldn't understand why he came here and why he stayed. They called me in to come down here since I'm from here and know the place."

"That makes little sense. Chris acted shocked when he saw me here. It seemed like a coincidence that we were both here."

"No. Camile was the one who found you and told him to come here. He didn't even know why he was coming here. He got in too deep with Camile."

My mother was the one behind it all. How could she do this? The sad thing is, I can actually see her doing this. I was nothing but a nuisance to her. "Did Chris tell you this right now?"

"Yeah. He's giving everything up. Poor guy got caught up with her and she turned him into something he wasn't."

I take a drink of water, stand up, and pace around. My adrenaline is pumping after discovering who was behind my life the last few years. To calm my adrenaline, I cross my arms in front of me and grip my chest.

"Chris started selling drugs to make a little extra cash on the side. Camile found out about him and knew where he lived. That must have been when she started her sick plan against you. After I left Sky Bar, I went to meet up with Cruz to catch up. We grew up together and were close, but I didn't want to stay here and he did, so we kept in touch. After dinner, we went back to his house since I've never seen it finished. We were only going to hang out and have a couple of beers. But when I saw you there, it made everything complicated. I didn't know it was you Cruz was talking about or vice versa. I could tell from talking to you at the bar that you really like someone. Then Cruz told me he met someone over dinner. That look in his eyes when he told me he met someone made me believe you're the one for him. You and Ashley were inside making drinks and I couldn't hold back and not tell Cruz anything. I felt so bad knowing what I knew and him falling for you. I wasn't sure if you were involved or not. I went against my job and told him what was going on."

I remember when they were talking outside; they were in deep conversation. That's when everything changed between Cruz and me. I never understood what had happened. "You sure did play it off well. I had no idea. I had a gut feeling something was off, but I didn't know what or why. So did Cruz end things on his terms?" I walk back over and take a seat. My nerves have calmed down enough for me to stop fidgeting and sit down.

"Not exactly. I did my research and couldn't come up with anything on you. I kept seeing Chris go to the same places you were at and couldn't understand why. Cruz knew nothing about your past, so we were at a dead end. I asked Cruz if he would end things with you so we could see if it opened up any doors to get to Camile. He didn't want to, but the more he saw Chris around, the more he wanted to know the truth. It took some time for him to agree."

"Wait, so he agreed, and what? You thought I would go running back to Chris? What was that going to tell you guys? Why didn't you ask me?"

"Because we still didn't know if you were behind any of this or not. We were so close to Camile I didn't want to risk losing her. We took a risk on that part to see what would happen. But the same thing happened. You weren't giving Chris the time or day when we saw you two together. So we knew you weren't a part of this." He leans in closer. "I owe Cruz big time for doing this for me. He knew he could risk losing you. You don't know how badly Cruz wanted to bash Chris's face in. I had to stop him a few times from going to look for Chris himself. I didn't want him to spook him and he'd run off."

"Did Cruz think I had anything to do with this?"

"No, he didn't. That's part of the reason it took him so long to agree to this. Cruz is a patient man. He waited it out as long as he could to see what was going on with you and Chris and if you would say anything to him, but you'd never open up."

"And Ashley? What was her involvement?" I question.

"She told me she knew nothing and didn't want to be involved. The only thing she agreed on is going along with me being a wilderness tour guide."

Ashley knew he was my ex, and she said nothing. She took my secret to heart when I told her I didn't want anyone to know.

"How did you guys set up the ambush? How did you guys know when my mom and Chris were going to come to my place?"

"We didn't. We always had eyes on Chris, but then Camile came into view and that's when we hurried and rounded everyone up. The minute we saw her, we didn't waste a second." He clears his throat. "Everyone knew you were innocent. I made sure they kept their hands off you."

I shake my head, taking everything in. "How did my mom become a drug mule?" I ask.

"My guess is she got in with the wrong people since she was doing drugs and one thing led to another. I'm actually shocked she used to be a drug addict because mules usually do it for the money and never care about the drugs. People who do drugs can't become mules because the drugs drag them back in. It surprised me that she kept clean being around drugs."

It's hard to take this all in. I'm happy Cruz wasn't involved with all this. It gives me hope there is still something there for us.

"What's going to happen to my mom and Chris?" I ask.

"Camile will spend the rest of her life in prison. Since this is Chris's first offense, the judge will order him to go to rehab. I know you haven't seen or spoken to your mom in a while. Would you like for me to set something up?"

"No," I say, shaking my head. "There is nothing I have to say to her. She said what she had to say earlier, and that is enough for me to know where her heart lies. Some things are better left unsaid."

"That's understandable," Brayden says and stands up. "Are you ready to get out of here? I think we've kept you long enough."

I get to my feet and head toward the entrance. Brayden comes to a halt and stares at me before opening the door.

"Trust me when I say this, Tessa. Cruz loves you. I saw the hurt on his face when he came to see me to tell me he ended it. I've never seen him look so hurt before, not even when his own dad passed away. Please don't take this out on him. We really had no clue who you were. You both deserve to be happy and you both give each other that happiness. Whatever happens when we walk out this door, please keep that in mind."

Taking hold of him, I wrap my arms around him. "Thank you for everything. I don't think I could have gotten away from Chris if it wasn't for you."

He squeezes me a little tighter. "Anytime."

We both exit the doorway and head to the front together. I hear yelling from one room and realize it's my mother. Brayden places his arm around my shoulders to comfort me as we pass the rooms where my mother and Chris are being held. In case I notice them, I keep my head down. I know I won't, but that's what feels right.

As Brayden's arm slips from my shoulder, I lift my head to see Cruz standing by the front door. His worried expression reveals how difficult this was for him. I feel Brayden's presence disappear. As I get closer to Cruz, I realize he's a little unsure about what the best step here is. I abruptly walk into him, wrapping my arms around him and pressing my face into his chest.

The tension I was holding onto releases. My arms become more relaxed. His touch helps center me. I feel at home in his arms. I raise my gaze toward him and mutter, "Take me home."

"Where's home?"

"Home is wherever you are."

He reaches for my chin and lifts my head. I rise on the balls of my feet and lean in for a kiss.

SIX MONTHS LATER...

Tessa

It's been six months since that shit went down. I'm kind of happy Chris came into my life. Without him, I would have never gotten my unanswered questions about my mom. Everything I have been through has made me into the person I am today.

Brayden was right. My mom got sentenced to life in prison and Chris went to rehab.

Cruz and I have talked about everything. I'm an open book now. He knows my life from the beginning until now. All his patience made me fall more and more in love with him each day that passes. He's the most patient man I have ever known. He wanted me to move in with him the day everything happened. I stayed at his house a lot for the first few weeks. But I needed to work on myself more before making that move. Everything was still so fresh and I was still trying to come to terms with it. He understood and told me whenever I was ready, he would be waiting. Cruz has never judged me for my past or treated me any differently after telling him everything. He treats me as he did before. He loves me even harder now that I could finally open up. It brought us closer together.

I asked Ashley why she said nothing to anyone about who Chris was. She said she kept her promise to keep my secret. I couldn't believe it. She allowed Cruz to break up with me and still stayed silent. She said she knew everything would turn out okay because she knew I was innocent.

After spending all day packing up my stuff to move in with Cruz, a knock comes on my door. Cruz said he wouldn't be by until tomorrow morning to help me move and drive the boxes over to his place. He mentioned a lot happening at the brewery. He needed to finish up before spending the weekend moving all my stuff to his place. Did he finish early and was here to surprise me?

Another knock comes through my front door. "Coming," I yell.

My whole body goes still. Confused, I remain frozen, staring at the person before me.

"Hi," he says.

Chris is standing at my doorway. But there is something different about him. His face has more color and his eyes are clearer. For once, his eyes aren't dilated and rapidly moving. His hair and facial hair have a nice clean cut. I'm staring at him in disbelief. He's gained back all the weight he lost. You wouldn't have been able to recognize the person he was six months ago.

"I know I'm the last person you expected. Can we talk?"

I'm in disbelief at him being here. I thought this was all over. He wasn't supposed to come back. He wasn't supposed to bother me anymore. Everything between us was a lie. There is nothing left. He takes a few steps closer to me and reaches out for my hand. I pull it away and feel throbbing throughout my whole body.

"Why are you here?" I yell.

His eyes go wide and he backs up. "Tessa. I promise I'm not here to start anything."

"Then why, Chris? Why are you here?" I'm so exhausted by him.

"I'm finished with rehab," he says and gives no other explanation.

My eyes are still fixed on him, waiting for him to go on.

"I'm not here to hurt you. I'm in a sober living house now and one requirement of living there is doing a twelve-step program. In the twelve-step program, I have to apologize to anyone I have hurt."

I stand here in silence, waiting for his apology. He backs away a little from the door and turns his back to me. His body shakes and a snort comes through him as if he's holding back his cries. I've never seen him cry before. I can't tell if this is fake or not. He turns to face me with tears running down his face. "I'm so sorry about everything I put you through. I know you have gone through a lot in your past and I didn't make it any better. I truly did love you. I still do. Despite the fucked-up things I did. But I know there is nothing left between us."

He tries to reach his hand out to me again, but I move back a little, still gripping the door.

"It doesn't matter anymore. Everything is over with. There is nothing left. I got my closure. You need to move on."

"I'm trying to, Tessa. I really am," he says and wipes away the tears streaming down his face. "This is why I'm here. I know there is nothing left for us, but for my closure, I had to come and apologize."

I loosen my grip on the door. I've trusted him too many

times. This time seems different. He seems different. I've never seen this side of him. Even when we first met. There is pain in his eyes I've never seen before. He's finally showing some guilt after all this time. "I know what drugs can do to someone. I've seen it happen. But I can't give you anything. I'm done with it all. I'm done with you."

"I'm not trying to get back with you, Tessa. I only want to have a conversation with you. I know I deserve nothing from you. Can we have one conversation? I'm sure you have questions for me. I have answers I can give you."

I snort out a laugh. "What makes you think I will believe anything you say to me? I know everything now. You weren't the only one being held up for questioning in a square cement room with one table." He appears surprised that I was questioned, too.

He looks down at his feet. "I'm sorry you had to go through that. I never expected any of this to happen."

"Then what did you expect when you were part of it all?"

He looks back up at me, shaking his head. "It was the drugs. They made me think and do things I never would have ever done. I was a different person. I didn't like that person. But I couldn't stop. I'm clean now. I promise. Please talk to me."

Am I stupid for wanting to hear all his pathetic excuses he's going to give me? Part of me wants to leave him down there. Another part wants to hear what he has to say. He's finally sober enough to have an adult conversation and maybe I can finally understand more from his point of view.

"Meet me downstairs while I go get my shoes on."

Nodding, he turns around and heads down.

Inhaling a large breath, I head downstairs. To my surprise, he's downstairs with water bottles and a backpack.

"What is this?" I ask.

"I wanted to see if you wanted to go on a hike while we talked?"

"What? No!" I give him a questioning look. I'm taken aback.

Since I've known him, he's never been active. He looks in better shape than he did when we first started dating.

"The sober living house has changed me a lot. Being active keeps my mind off the addiction. Talking about this makes me anxious. It will help keep my mind off it while we talk. I promise I'm not doing anything deceiving. You can stay behind me if that makes you feel safer."

"Fine. Where to?"

His face lights up after I agree to this. I hope I don't regret it.

"There's this spot I found that overlooks the entire town. It's pretty cool. The hike is a little rough, so I brought some water and snacks. I also have a first aid kit."

My eyebrows rise in surprise. He really is different. Even a little more cheerful. "Let's go," I say as I walk off from him.

I hear him shuffling his feet behind me.

We finally made it to the top of the cliff. Neither of us talked because of how rough this hike was. At least he was honest about something. My back is toward Chris while I stand here, trying to catch my breath. And that moment was another mistake I made because everything goes black.

I'm seeing stars above my head. The day has ended and the night sky has rolled in. The shuffling noise coming behind me brings me back to the reality of what happened. Chris hit me and knocked me out. Turning my head over to the left, I see Chris pacing around in circles, talking to himself.

As I reach around, feeling for a rock I can hold in my hand in case he tries to hit me again, I hurry and stand up.

"What the fuck is wrong with you? I see you haven't changed, you stupid bastard."

Chris turns around, facing me with his hands up in the air.

"I wanted you to see what you've done to me. Look at me," he says with his hands running down his body. "I'm not the same and I will never be the same. My skin crawls twenty-four seven. I can't make it stop."

"You did this to yourself," I say.

Ignoring me, he kneels down and opens the backpack. "If it weren't for your stupid mother and you, none of this would've ever happened." He pulls out a syringe, a small plastic Ziplock bag, a spoon, and a lighter.

"You brought me up here to watch you shoot up. Shoot up for all I care. I don't give a shit. Stop blaming everyone else for your problems."

I watch as he lights up the spoon to heat his drug of choice. He takes the syringe, pulls back the plunger, and empties the spoon. "All I can think about is this. It consumes my life now. You're going to watch what you did to me," he says in a shaky voice.

Within thirty seconds, he rips off his belt, ties it around his left arm, and shoots up. The second he empties the syringe into his vein, a sigh comes out of him and a relief comes on his face that I've never seen before. He gradually lays himself down on his left side, staring at me. Until his eyes look so heavy, he finally closes them.

I can't believe he wanted me to watch this. I grew up watching my mother and all her boyfriends on drugs. Never did I ever see it in action. This shit knocks you out as fast as anesthesia. I stand here, debating what I should do next. He deserves to rot up here.

I walk over to him and give him a shove with my foot to see if he's really out. His body is limp, and he rolls over onto his back. Hovering over him, I watch to see if any movement comes from him. He doesn't make a move. All I see is the slight movement in his chest. I turn my back on him with the rock and water bottle still in my hand and head back down.

Cruz and I walk into the brewery with our hands entwined with each other. We finally got all my stuff moved into his place. I had little, so it didn't take long. What took long was deep cleaning the studio after everything was out. Plus, working on top of that.

I slide into the booth and Cruz slides in right next to me. I wrap my arm around his and let out a long yawn as I lay my head on his shoulder. He kisses the top of my head. "If you're tired, we can tell Brayden to do this tomorrow."

Brayden had called Cruz and asked if we would have dinner with him. My stomach sank when Cruz told me. It's been a few days since I've seen Chris. I haven't heard anything either. Cruz doesn't know what happened that night. I feel so stupid for letting myself go with him. We've been so busy too that it slipped my mind. Which I'm thankful for. I wanted to get myself situated before telling him what happened. I'm still trying to figure out what happened myself.

We don't know what Brayden wants. He wouldn't say over the phone. He came into town last night. Didn't even say if it was for business or not. I can only assume it has something to do with Chris. Maybe he was lying about being done with rehab. It was part of his sentencing. Is he coming to warn us? Too late. I've already been warned.

"Hey," Brayden says and pats Cruz on the back.

I lift my head off Cruz's shoulder and watch as Brayden sits in front of us. "Hi, Brayden."

"Hey, man. What's going on?" Cruz asks.

"Hi, Cruz. Are you guys ready to order?" the new waitress says. She's new to town, and Cruz hired her after Ashley wanted to be a bartender. When I found out she was new, I wondered what her story was. I always wonder what everyone's story is now.

Ashley appears by Brayden's side just as we are done putting in our order. "Why didn't anyone tell me you guys were coming in?" She looks between Cruz and me and then at Brayden. "When did you get here?"

All of us stay quiet. Me and Cruz don't even know what is going on.

"Can you give us a minute, Ashley?" Brayden says.

She eyes us all, brows furrowed. "What's going on? Is everything okay?"

I shrug in question. "We actually don't know."

Brayden lets out a sigh. "It has to do with Chris."

My stomach drops. I look up at Cruz, but he doesn't look a bit surprised. Do they know I was with him?

Brayden squints his eyebrows and looks between Cruz and me. "Is there something I don't know?"

We both look at each other and then back at him. "No," Cruz says. Does he know something, and he's waiting for me to come clean?

Ashley steps out of the booth. "I'll give you guys a minute."

The waitress comes and places our drinks on the table. She must notice our expressions. She gives us a small grin and walks away.

Brayden clears his voice. "Have any of you heard from Chris?"

Unconsciously, I shake my head. I've been trying so hard to wash that day out of my mind. Brayden is eyeing us both, waiting for us to say more.

"I don't know how else to say this," he mutters.

"Just get to it, Brayden. Stop acting like we're in questioning," Cruz says.

Brayden takes a drink of his beer. "We found Chris at the bottom of a cliff."

I rush my hands to my mouth, holding in what's trying to come up.

"Are you okay?" Cruz rubs my back as I try to stop the heaving.

Nodding, I wipe the tears from my face. Brayden comes back with a glass of water and sets it in front of me. "Thank you." I reach for the cup and take a slow sip.

"I'm guessing no one knew he was back in town?" Brayden asks.

What happened after I left? I didn't think he would die. Should I have helped him? I wrap my arms around my stomach, trying to stop the unsettling feeling. Cruz wraps his arm around me and I scoot a little closer to him.

"Do you guys know what happened?" Cruz asks.

"We believe he overdosed and rolled off the cliff." Brayden eyes Cruz like there is something there between them that only the two of them know. "The same cliff."

Cruz nods.

The same cliff? What cliff?

"You two know nothing about this? He didn't contact you, Tessa?"

"No," I mumble.

The waitress comes back over and sets our plates down.

"I'm sorry. We need to-go boxes."

The waitress smiles at Cruz and walks away.

She's a very quiet one. But I was also quiet when I first got here. It's intimidating starting over in a new town and not knowing anyone.

"What happened to his rehab?" I ask.

Brayden takes a bite of his burger as if this isn't affecting him. He must be used to this. "He finished his six months there and went to a sober living house. Then I got the call that he was found at the bottom of the cliff. His case has now reopened."

"Reopened? Is that bad?" I ask.

"If there was evidence of foul play, but we didn't find any. It's common for someone to overdose right after rehab. Their body isn't used to the amount of drugs they used to take before they became clean. But they don't know that. So a lot of times they take the same amount they used to take. It looks like that's what Chris did and probably passed out too close to the edge."

Cruz packs up our food in our to-go boxes. I didn't even realize they were brought over. Cruz has been quiet this whole time. I'm not sure if he doesn't know what to say or if he doesn't care.

"That's why I wanted to talk to you to see if he contacted you to piece together why he came back here. I'm sure he came back here for you." Brayden looks at me. "A lot of times when someone gets clean, they have a lot of remorse for what they did."

I know that wasn't it. It doesn't matter anymore. He's no longer here. They found no evidence of foul play. So there's no reason to say anything. Deep down, he still had demons he couldn't fight. Demons he wanted to blame me for. If I didn't let my mother blame me for hers, I will not let him.

Forbidden Secrets are better left unsaid.

There comes a time when you have to take matters into your own hands to save the ones you love. I never thought I'd be in this position again. The thing people don't know about this town is, secrets are held onto longer than relationships.

My mother was a victim of abuse at the hands of the man she loved. She loved my dad even after all the abuse she received from him. Day after day, we watched him drown himself in some sort of drug. He never used the same drug, so it was hard to tell what he was on. Pretty soon, we figured it out by the way the drugs affected him. Sometimes he slept for weeks on end, and those were the days we prayed for. Some days he was so strung out he didn't know what to do with himself. Those were the days we dreaded. He would get so strung out he didn't know where to put all his energy. So, of course, the easiest person he had around to take his energy out on was his wife.

Shockingly, he never came after me. I learned to keep out of his way the days he was using. So did my mother, but at times it only made things worse.

We kept this all a secret. My mother always said after every bruise. "Please don't tell anyone, sweetie. No one will understand. He needs to get better first." She didn't want anyone to know her husband, the father of her child, was an abusive drug addict. She asked me to promise I would take it to my grave.

I don't remember when this first happened. It became the norm for our family. A way of life we had to learn to live. I remember my mom spending hours in front of the mirror covering up her bruises. She became pretty good at it. Sometimes I didn't know where the bruises were. No one else did either. No one asked. No one questioned.

Everyone thought we were this happy family. And we were sometimes. Every time my dad was sober, he looked at the aftermath of the house, my mom, and he would beg for forgiveness. Then he would join meetings again. But he made sure his meetings were hours away from here, so he wouldn't run into anyone he knew. Not only did we keep this a secret, but he did too.

Cruz, it's because he's not in his right mind. He's sick. He needs to get better. Are the words that always ran through my head growing up. When does the better come? When does someone finally reach their breaking point? I could tell when my mom finally reached her breaking point. I could see it, I could feel it, but she never knew a way out. A permanent way out. She knew he would torment us till the day he was in his own grave.

Once I hit my teens, I was stronger, and I would try to protect my mother. Sometimes it helped and he would stop. Sometimes all I did was make it worse for her. I had to learn when to step in and when not to. There were countless nights I cried, not being able to help her out like I wanted to. Especially since I was older and stronger.

Then came a time when they both hid it from me. It was easy because I went to school all day and then spent my evenings working at the local grocery store. I was gone all day long, giving my dad the time he needed to do what he wanted. He learned my schedule and so in return, he learned to hold off on my days off. Since my mom was very good at hiding the bruises and redecorating the house, it was hard for me to tell when it happened. A lot of times, I thought he was doing better. When I would question my mom if he was doing better, she would say he was. Like all the other lies, that was a lie too.

There are a lot of high rocky areas around here where one stupid move could cost you your life. There was a spot my dad took me to growing up. If you were careful enough and you had an off-road vehicle, you could drive to it. My dad was really good at off-roading. He grew up doing this as a hobby. Putting hours on end fixing up his jeep and learning how to climb the rocks. On his good days, we would go off-roading. We found a spot we called *ours*. A very steep narrow spot that not many people came to. Either because no one knew about it or couldn't get up it. Many tried and failed. It was also a good hiking spot to sit and stare out over the horizon. It made me feel so tall, like I could do anything in the world and become anything I wanted to become. Over the years, fewer people came to this spot because of how dangerous it was. Over time, the relationship between my dad and me drifted further and further away until it was nonexistent. But I always hiked our spot if I needed time to myself. It was the best spot to get away from everything and think clearly.

One day after a long Thursday night at home, which turned into an even longer Friday at school and work, I took a hike up to my favorite spot, not knowing what I was going to find. I found my dad's jeep sitting at the edge of the cliff. The car was off and so were the lights. I was confused at first because I didn't think he came here anymore. I hadn't seen him come back to this spot in years. He had the car seat down all the way and he was lying there asleep, or so I thought until I saw the needle sticking out of his vein and his belt wrapped around his arm.

Without even thinking, the next move I made was unthinkable. But one I don't regret. I reached down to his right foot and pushed it down on the gas pedal as far down as his foot would go. I started the engine and put the car in neutral. Throwing myself away from the car, I watched it slowly roll off the cliff. I sat there, waiting for the hit from the bottom to come. Once it finally did, I booked it out of there as quickly as I could, taking another way down that led me to the back of the cliff. From there, I took the long way home.

Saturday morning, a cop came knocking on our door. A knock I expected to happen sooner or later. My mom opened the door and, like always, played dumb, like everything was right with our family. Right after they told her they found her husband dead at the bottom of a cliff, she broke out in a hysterical cry. A cry I knew was fake. I saw her cry too many times to count, and this was not her normal cry. The cops chalked it up to an overdose and he must have left his car running when he started overdosing and rolled it over the cliff. No investigation was held and hardly any questions were asked. The funeral happened and ended quicker than a cheetah after its prey. We finally got to live our lives the way it should have been. *Happy*.

I still hike to the same spot every so often. Usually when I need time to think or get away. I had a lot to do at the brewery and told Tessa I would see her in the morning and we would start moving all her stuff to our home. Everything that has happened over the past six months has made my past resurface more than I ever imagined it would. I will do anything to keep Tessa safe. Just as I did with my mom.

To my surprise, when I got to the top of the cliff, I saw another person. Who would be up here at this time? It was almost midnight, and nobody hiked this part anymore. As I walked closer, this person already looked dead. He was lying there on the edge of the cliff with hardly any movement in his chest. I didn't know who it was until I was standing over him. Chris. Tessa's ex-boyfriend. Then the same images I'd kept buried away for the past twenty years flooded back to my mind. A syringe hung out of his vein, with a belt wrapped around his arm.

Like I did years ago when I did the unthinkable, I rolled him off the cliff. I didn't wait this time to hear him hit the bottom. I turned and walked away.

Déjà vu hit me when I took the same trail back home I'd taken twenty years ago.

Sometimes you have to do the unthinkable in order to keep your loved ones safe. And like my mother always told me when the town found out about my dad, *promise me you will take this to the grave. It's our secret. No one can find out your dad was abusive. They already know he was a sick man and abused drugs. Promise me, Cruz. Promise me you will keep this a secret and take it to your grave.*

I've kept my mom's secrets after all these years. I've also kept my own secret to myself. No one knew it was me who rolled my dad off the cliff, just like no one will know I rolled Chris off the cliff.

Like I have for many years, I will continue to take these *forbidden secrets* to my grave.

ABOUT

Mia enjoys spending time with her husband and two spoiled dogs. When she's not home reading, writing, or binge-watching shows, she's traveling the world and spends every chance she can get outdoors in the summertime.

Website:
https://www.authormiaskye.com/
Goodreads:
https://www.goodreads.com/author/show/22332113.Mia_Skye
Facebook:
https://www.facebook.com/authormiaskye/
Instagram:
author.miaskye
TikTok:
https://www.tiktok.com/@authormiaskye

ALSO BY

Whoever said marriage is bliss clearly wasn't talking about my marriage. I'm on vacation with my husband in an attempt to save our marriage.

I expected to be wined and dined, treated like a queen, and to rekindle our dying spark. Instead, I walked in on my husband cheating on me in our hotel room.

Still reeling from finding my two-timing husband in bed with someone else, I meet a man who seems too good to be true—and he's all too willing to help take my mind off my failed marriage.

But something this perfect can't possibly come out of this disaster of a vacation…can it?

Now that I've developed an unexpected love with someone new, my deceptive husband is back. He has one goal in mind…to win back my love.

Wrapped up in uncertainties and unknowns…which decision should I make? And when I come to terms with the right decision…will it be too late?

———————

You can order *Ever After* on Amazon today!

Read for free in Kindle Unlimited.